Spooks

Anthology for the Olga Sinclair Open Short Story Competition 2019

Compiled and edited by Kathy Joy

Acknowledgements

The Norwich Writers' Circle would like to thank our adjudicators, Piers Warren and Holly Ainley for their stellar judging. With so many amazing entries, we know it can't have been easy!

We'd also like to thank Black Shuck Gin Ltd for sponsoring our competition. Not only did they run a free gin tasting at the launch gala, but they generously donated prizes for the ten finalists.

http://blackshuckltd.co.uk/

Finally, we would finally like to express our gratitude to everyone who entered the competition and to the winning authors for allowing us to showcase their stories in this anthology.

CONTENTS

Winners

Shortlisted

Members Challenge Shield

A Tribute to Olga Sinclair

By Anne Funnell

Olga Sinclair passed away on April 28th, 2014, aged 91.

She left us a surprise legacy in her will. This donation to our funds has supported our annual Open Prose Competition ever since. For the benefit of those reading this anthology who may not know anything about her, I have been asked to write an introduction.

Olga joined the Norwich Writers' Circle in 1960, aged 37. Within seven years, she had published her first book for children with Blackwell's, followed by 4 others. She published 25 books altogether under the names of Ellen Clare, Olga Daniels, and her married name of Olga Sinclair, with several other publishers, depending on the genre. She wrote romantic historical fiction sticking as far as possible to the facts, which she meticulously researched. I remember her telling me of a visit to Scotland, and the book she wrote afterwards called, *Gretna Green* (A romantic History). The last book she wrote was called *The Countess and the Miner*, published in 2005 by Robert Hale.

For Poppyland she wrote two historical books, *When Wherries Sailed By* (1987) and *Potter Heigham (The Heart of Broadland)* (1989).

She acted as Magistrate for several years, giving her an understanding of current affairs and local issues.

In 1968 she became a committee member for the Circle, and she was the Hon Treasurer for a couple of years. She became Vice-President in 1980. After Mary Ingate died in 1991, she was elected as President in 1992. She remained a loyal and hard-working member, graciously handing over the trophies at our annual prize-givings, until the AGM of July 2012, after which she felt unable to continue.

She was a member of the Romantic Novelists Association, and encouraged me to attend meetings in London, and we went together to conferences which took place in University buildings during the summer vacations from 1992 to 2005.

We had more than one garden party at their Dove House Farm in Potter Heigham.

Her husband, Stanley, who sadly predeceased her, had a very quirky sense of humour for a headmaster of Thorpe School, Norwich. He organised one quiz where we had to identify monstrous or down-right odd "ornaments" he had carved and constructed in his garden. One I remember was a yellow "Marigold", which was a rubber washing-up-glove suddenly rising up out of the pond on a pneumatic blast set off by a time-switch.

Olga enjoyed country dancing, and when widowed attended dances with her dancing partner and chauffeur, Charles. Her friends from the group attended her funeral and afterwards performed dances for us, thus making this the jolliest funeral I have ever attended.

Olga embodied in her warmth and humour the aim of the

founding members of the Circle, in 1943, "To encourage the art and craft of writing and promote good fellowship amongst Norfolk and Norwich writers generally."

Foreword

Piers Warren

What a treat to be allowed to read 127 brand new stories in my favourite genre – spooks! So, first I'd like to say a huge thank you to The Norwich Writers' Circle for inviting me to judge this year's competition, and to all the authors who put so much effort into their submissions.

I know how much hard work it can be to produce both short and novel-length fiction so I felt sorry for the 117 who didn't make it into the top ten. But rest assured, I read every single entry from start to finish and they were all worth it. My method was that as I read each one I gave it a rough score and added some comments on a spreadsheet, that I could refer to later, and initially whittled it down to twenty outstanding pieces. I then read all those again and chose my top ten, by which time it was pretty clear in my mind which would come in first, second and third. Overall I was very impressed with the quality of writing and would love to read more from a number of the authors. In fact several of the submissions felt like great starting points to develop into a full novels.

Although the entries were received over a period of a few months, in general those received nearer the deadline were better. That might suggest that the more time you have to write, edit and tweak your story the better, but it is certainly not a rule and indeed the first prize winner was one of the early ones I read. I received about ten submissions printed out on paper but interestingly none of those made it into my top twenty. I'm not sure we can analyse that but there seems to be no benefit to entering on paper rather than as a Word document.

As for the word count, that did not seem to affect the quality of the finished product. All were over a thousand words and some of my favourites were actually at the lower end – the third prize going to a story of just over 1,300 words, for example. The majority of entries submitted had a word count of exactly 2,000 or just a few words less, suggesting that initial drafts were over the limit and were then whittled down with a number of edits to become eligible. But when you consider that out of my top twenty favourites only seven or eight were this close to the limit, that leads me to think that this is not always the best approach. If your story feels complete, yet is a few hundred words or so less than the top limit I say go for it as it is. Certainly don't feel you have to pad things out to come close to the total number of words allowable.

The theme of 'spooks' can be interpreted in various ways of course, all allowed in the rules of the competition, though as expected the vast majority dealt with matters that were ghostly in some way. One used 'spook' as the slang term for a black person, an ethnic slur dating back to the 1940s, and about ten had their spooks as spies. One of the runners up had a spy theme – but with a modern twist that the protagonist was an undercover police officer sent in to infiltrate possible terrorists over a long period of time. It's also a love story and a very memorable piece, nearly making it into the top three. I'm sure you'll enjoy reading it in the anthology.

Some of the stories managed to create a spooky atmosphere without necessarily featuring or mentioning ghosts. Our third prize-winner is a good example of this. And quite a few used the common technique of revealing right at the very end that one of the key characters had been a ghost all along. About four of my top ten did this but it has to be dealt with carefully so it's not a let down or a cop out. In the same way that ending a fantastical story by saying 'then I woke up and realised it had all been a dream' can be deeply unsatisfactory. Surprise endings are not necessary, our superb second prize-winner introduced the ghost in the very first sentence.

Of course, you can write, read and enjoy a spooky ghost story whether you believe in ghosts or not. But, as with writing science fiction, the more techniques you can use to draw in the reader the better, especially if they are non-believers! It was interesting to note that out of my top ten choices only two of them were not written in the first person. I think this is one of those techniques, it being somehow more direct and believable when someone grabs you by the lapel and says 'I'm terrified – let me tell you why', rather than a third person narrative told by an outsider looking in.

This is connected to my love of how stories start; the first sentences used to pull the reader in. When you're writing a short story you don't have the luxury of lengthy scene-setting descriptions or character development so can cut to the chase straight away. I'd like to share with you a few of my favourite opening lines from this year's competition. Our first prize-winner starts with 'That eerie sound echoed over the dark water again last night...' immediately creating atmosphere and anticipation. The second prize-winner has 'I fell in love with a ghost' an intriguing set up in the first person, and one of the runners up starts with 'Once, I did a heinous thing.' This is followed by 'I don't expect you to love me or even to feel sorry for me but it will help me in my tormented state if I can be certain you will read my story.' A good example of the lapel-grabbing technique.

I do hope you enjoy reading the anthology as much as I have enjoyed reading all submissions, and thanks again to The Norwich Writers' Circle and all the entrants.

WINNERS

1st Place

The Serenity of Still Water

By Iain Andrews

That eerie sound echoed over the dark water again last night…

As if something damp is slapping against the boards of the walkway…

At first I considered an otter or a mink, but the rhythm is too slow. More akin to footsteps, although what makes them I dare not contemplate.

I detest this lonely dwelling in the Norfolk Broads and am resolved to leave tomorrow. My friend Jennifer joined me for the first week but she's left me alone. I blame no-one but myself for my torment. I told everyone I wanted solitude. I didn't want reminders of Keith's death—strangers approaching me with false condolences, the correspondence bearing his name dropping through the letter box, the empty chair in the lounge, the coldness of the other side of the bed.

Perhaps I'm still in denial. Anger and depression lurk before I can break free of my grief. The Law also denies his passing. I'll endure a wait of seven years unless the sea surrenders his corpse to the shore or he's snared in a fishing net.

I don't want to stay here anymore, but I dread my return to the city. The restaurants, the theatres, the bars—places where Keith and I shared an intimate joy his passing has ripped forever from my life. I'll endure the sneering accusations of his friends and family: how I held him back; how he could have done a lot better; how he never really drank before he met me. They will not utter it but their eyes will scream I killed him.

I'll have to deal with the financial repercussions of his death as well as face an inquest where they'll force me to relive the events that took his life. I've already related my account of that horrific night several times to the police and coastguards.

I'll testify about the yachting holiday with Jennifer and her husband when Keith slipped overboard after dark. The boom must have swung across and struck him because the sail wasn't properly fastened—no point asking me the technical details. We'd all had a bit too much booze. His final scream will haunt me forever. We searched for him until exhaustion and an angry sea extinguished hope. Keith was the only sailor among us. The holiday was his idea. God knows how we managed to steer the boat back into port.

Jennifer was amazing. When I spotted this place on the internet she agreed to join me for a few days to help me settle in. She even promised to keep it a secret from everyone, even her husband, so I wouldn't be bothered. I reckon she was glad to get away from him—their marriage was on the rocks but she never told me why.

The house is unique. It's a converted boat-shed on stilts, connected to land by a long wooden boardwalk. The structure sits in a private broad, so no pleasure boats disturb the calm waters that embrace it. It has no electricity or a phone line, and neither can I receive a mobile signal.

It was perfect during the early days of autumn. I sat on the small deck under an endless sky with a bottle of wine and listened to the birdsong and the gentle murmur of the breeze through the reeds. The water entranced me—I could watch nothing but the gentle ripples for hours. There was a sense of timelessness, of otherworldliness, letting me imagine I inhabited a land where the torment of my memories was a bad dream.

Now the days are nothing more than a respite from my fears, a chance to drown my despair in tears and alcohol.

It's these nights I really dread. Perhaps I'm not used to loneliness, but I staywwww indoors and bolt the door.

The noises started as soon as Jennifer left. Not that there weren't sounds late at night before then—the call of birds, revelry from a distant cruiser—but it was my first night alone when I heard the birds call in alarm before those steady muted beats. I called out, thinking someone approached but received no answer except the mocking whistle of the wind. I dared to look out the window, but the cold light of the waning moon revealed nothing but the reeds standing like a besieging army.

The boardwalk passes through the reeds, then crosses an area of carr, a dank foetid swamp where the limbs of dying trees point in every direction like skeletal arms. When I arrived, I saw it as a vision of Purgatory, a place where my soul would transit from the world I knew to the paradise beyond. Perhaps I thought then the boathouse was a manifestation of that heaven, but now, when the sun sets, it becomes the opposite.

The wooden pathway emerges onto a dirt track, at the side of which lie the ruins of an abandoned church, nothing more than the remains of four low walls and a column of masonry, once part of the steeple, pointing like a defiant finger towards heaven. The village beyond is small, consisting of a few flint-clad houses, an old pub and a convenience store. Jennifer and I spent a couple of drunken evenings in the tavern. Transitory tourists ensure it is full throughout the summer months but in these darkening days its clientele is reduced to a few taciturn locals. The landlord and his wife are pleasant enough, but the old men who sit clutching their pints in the dark corners under ancient scarred beams do not welcome strangers.

Two of them tried to intimidate us.

'Don't tarry near the old church,' one said. 'It's haunted.'

'Worse than that,' said the other. 'The bishop did too good a job. When he deconsecrated it or something. Took more'n the holiness out of the place.'

The first man nodded. 'Left it to the Devil. They say it be the gateway to Hell now.'

We smiled, although we increased our pace as we tottered past the ruin on our return. The incident unsettled me, but not Jennifer. Confidence is her middle name. A bit like Keith. I've always been attracted to self-assured people. I need them, if truth be told. Sadly, they seldom reciprocate. Keith and Jennifer were the only ones who made any effort to make me feel wanted.

The day after I first heard the noise, I returned to the village. The old church seemed darker than before, and I thought I saw movement in the shadows by the far wall. I wasn't nervous, at least not of any supernatural presence. I suspected my nocturnal visitor was a local, and the reason for my trip was to purchase some fishing line.

On my return I strung a length of this across the boardwalk and attached several empty tin cans. Should a trespasser approach in the dark my improvised alarm would alert me and with any luck deter any further intrusion. I sat down with a glass of Merlot and waited, fearful about what I could do if my stalker tried to enter the house.

That sound came again, preceded by the wildfowl's cacophony, but not accompanied by rattling cans. Hoping whatever made it offered no danger, I crept out with a torch. The night was clear after a dry day, and the pale moonlight was enough to reveal what looked like footprints crossing the boards. It was as if more than one person had emerged from the reeds on one side and walked back into the broad a few feet closer to my door. I attempted to reassure myself that this was some natural phenomenon—perhaps a shoal of fish had leapt from

17

the water and flopped their way back to their normal habitat. The sound of something moving in the water nearby may have given credence to this theory—it didn't reduce my growing sense of dread, the certainty that someone was watching me.

An unearthly glow shimmered through the reeds close by—not a torch or headlights, but more ethereal. At first I put it down to fireflies but the faint white glow moved away too smoothly.

Since then I have heard the sound six times, including last night. I know that the wildfowl do not screech because I am near. Their cries begin before that awful sound, and reverberate across the marshes long after whatever made it have gone. Each time the sound itself is louder, as if whatever makes it draws closer to where I shiver in my chair.

Last night I detected a subtle change in the sounds from the marsh. The birds shrieked as before, but the unnerving flapping, for I can think of no better word, was joined by what seemed a whisper, not the soft whistling of the wind through the bulrushes, but something akin to voices, soft yet angry.

I sensed changes in pitch, almost as if two entities were murmuring in union as they moved between wood and water.

And now, I sit staring out of the window, a glass of wine in my trembling hand. Its colour reminds me of blood. Dusk is falling and I curse the indecision that forced me to stay for one more day. I could leave immediately but that would mean walking through the carr to the ruined church before I could obtain a phone signal. And there is something terrifying about that lonely spot when night falls. In my brief spells of fitful sleep, I dream the devil is waiting for me within its crumbling walls.

In spite of the chilling breeze, a low mist has formed inland and is creeping towards the house.

The ducks and geese are stirring.

The mist begins to swirl, and the faint glow grows closer

and brighter. The birds' calls recede and I realise they are deserting me. The calm water now speaks of the death of the wind, the unbending reeds suggesting even time has ceased to flow. The air is humid and heavy, the way it feels when a terrible storm is building.

A deathly silence now smothers the Broad.

I wish Jennifer was still here.

But in a way she is.

I rolled her battered body off the deck outside, weighted down by stones I took from that cursed churchyard. I discovered she and Keith were lovers, and my wrath could not be soothed even by his death. She never suspected I murdered him as well, consigning his body to rot in the depths of the ocean before I loosened the mast.

And now all I can do is cower, alone with my guilt and fear. But this torturous solitude cannot last. The lights and the mist outside creep closer.

I watch as they coalesce into two familiar figures rising from the Broad. They hold hands but their free arms are beckoning me to join them.

As they advance towards me I sense their unspoken promise that my grief and anger will only be abated when we three are reconciled in the serenity of still water.

Adjudicators comments: Although I came across this story fairly early on in my delightful task of reading all the submissions, I immediately knew it was top notch and would be hard to beat. I was right! Supremely well written in a style that is both engaging and feels natural, the author wastes no time in building suspense – 'eerie' being the second word in the piece. The writing is very evocative and descriptive – it's easy for the reader to picture the scene and hear the sounds – and I could remember the setting well, long after I had read

19

it. The first person narrator is staying in an idyllic setting and yet is clearly unhappy, so you long to find out why. You soon do, or at least think you do, but the gripping story has various twists to come. Half way through you think the main spooky element is being introduced, but this is just a side-track, while the tension builds until a series of surprises ends the story in a spookily satisfactory way. The description of how a seemingly respectable and ordinary life can hide the anguish of trauma is cleverly treated. I would happily read a novel-length version of this story and hope to come across more from this author. Congratulations to a very worthy winner.

2ⁿᵈ Place

Cornelia

by Joseph Tipgrave

I fell in love with a ghost. I'm not a man of profligate emotions. My friends will tell you that I am guarded, restrained; not lacking in warmth but slow to open up to new people. Yet, in my middle years, I find myself confronting those two staple questions: do you believe in love at first sight? Do you believe in ghosts?

Yes. To both. It cannot be denied that there's something sexy about the incorporeal, an allure in the insubstantial that cannot be matched by flesh and blood. To be specific, ghosts are better than living humans at the following:

Whispering sweet nothings in your ear.

Running fingers up and down your spine.

Sustaining meaningful silences.

Making flowers wilt in a vase (something to appeal to the goth sensibility).

Being fascinating and diaphanous in the moonlight.

And, if that were not enough, on sultry nights they can chill a room to perfection.

These are attributes that would not appeal to the modern romantic sensibility. A ghost won't ride behind you on the mudguard of a bicycle as you freewheel down a hill on a summer's afternoon. And there'll be no tumbling over and over, laughing, in a snow drift, or declarations of undying love under torrents of rain. Ghosts don't buy presents or prepare romantic meals, and if you upset them they'll fill the house with black, buzzing flies until the foul mood passes.

The biggest drawback is telling your parents.

I came out to my family as gay when I was in my mid-thirties. By then my mother – a soap opera obsessive – had invested herself emotionally in a dozen storylines featuring winsome young men, so she was, if anything, pleased by my revelation. I left her with the sticky business of telling my father.

The scriptwriters of *Eastenders*, for all their diversity, sensitivity and radical tendencies are not yet ready to introduce a story of love across the eternal divide. There's be no spectral hand reaching longingly from the vast realm of night to find its fleshy counterpart. No sound of foot on stirrup as the lovers ride away from Albert Square, the horse's pale flank pierced by bloody spurs. The BBC is not yet ready for ghost-love, I feel sure. Nor yet, my mother.

In truth, I haven't even told my closest friends. My beloved and I have been secret lovers for a year now. It is time for my friends to come and meet her.

The invitations have been issued. There's no point in delaying further. My friends thought that since I moved into this prim Edwardian villa I have been reclusive and solitary. They have regularly expressed concern.

I have been anything but solitary. My darling is called Cornelia Wallington. She was a suffragette and died in this very house after being released from prison. Her death was caused by complications following the ill treatment she suffered during incarceration. This was hushed up, of course.

I am the only man she has ever been in love with.

From the first, I never felt alone in this house. I'd catch the sound of a footfall on the stairs, a sigh from an unlit corner, the sudden billowing of a curtain on a windless night. A whispering breath on my cheek as I fell asleep, and the smell of violets.

It was several weeks later that I first saw her, standing silent and gaunt at the end of my bed, a frosty patch of moonlight on her cheek.

I said it was love at first sight, and so it was. I was frozen with fear certainly, but irrevocably hooked. How long she stood there gazing into my eyes, I can't recall. Perhaps it was all night. At dawn, she was gone.

After that, she appeared most evenings. Sometimes, I would feel her slender fingers on my neck, or her lips would touch my ear. Once I felt her whole body in my arms, insistent and bony, like a precarious pile of books I couldn't quite hold on to.

Most evenings, we would sit together. She never spoke, but I knew her thoughts; a tender, solemn contralto sounded in my head. Over time I learned her story, and she mine.

That's another advantage of the dead over the living: they offer serenity, undemanding companionship, order. When I lived with Barney I would despair at the untidiness, the unemptied ashtrays and half-finished crosswords, the tardiness and the casual dishonesty that marks human love. At times Barney smelled as though he had been expelled from the grave.

John and Daniel arrived first, holding out a bottle of Prosecco and a box of organic mint chocolates.

"All the way from Walthamstow," said John. "The tube was a nightmare. Better get that wine poured."

As they crossed the threshold, my stomach lurched. No visitors had been since Cornelia's appearance. How would my guests respond to her? How would she feel about these strangers? Perhaps I shouldn't have asked so many, but it made sense to get the introductions over in one go. And so, Beverley and Fran arrived, grumbling about their babysitter. Barney appeared at the same time as Lawrence and Daisy. We were eight and would soon be nine.

The guests gathered in the sitting room. Barney lingered for a moment in the hallway and squeezed my hand. "You ok, pet?" There was concern in his blue eyes. We hugged. He was warm and had put on a little weight. We joined the other guests.

"Is the rumour, true?" asked Daisy as I handed round glasses of Prosecco.

"What rumour," I asked. I took a long pull on my own glass. I needed to calm my nerves.

"There's somebody new in your life. Someone special?"

Time to get it over with. "Yes. That's right," I said.

"About time, too," called Daniel. "You were turning back into a virgin."

Daisy directed a disapproving frown at Daniel. "That's nice to hear," she said. "So when does he arrive. We're dying to meet him."

"Well, it's not exactly a man."

There was a good deal of laughter, even from Daisy. My cheeks felt hot. I avoided looking at Barney.

"I knew it. I told John, didn't I? I said it would be a tranny. You were always the type. A bit too butch to be a proper poof, so you've turned to boys in fishnets."

"Shut up, Danny," said Beverley.

"Ooh if looks could kill."

"When is she arriving?" said Beverley.

"Yes," said Daisy. "We're longing to meet her."

The others expressed similar sentiments. The air grew thick with female pronouns.

They waited for my answer. In the silence, a blackbird sang from my back garden. This was usually the signal for dusk, and for Cornelia to arrive. Moths tapped like tiny knuckles on the window pane.

"She's coming," I said, my voice husky.

Fran said, "You should have asked her here earlier, so that she doesn't have to walk in on a crowded room. Very intimidating meeting us lot in one go." She winked.

"She always comes at this time."

I opened another bottle and walked around the room refilling glasses. The conversation slowly started up again. Beverley said, "Is she coming on the trains? They've been very bad the past couple of weeks."

The blackbird stopped singing. The sinking sun cast amber light and shifting wisteria shadows into the room. And there was Cornelia, in the dark corner between the door and window, her hands, white as two lilies, clasped at her waist; her eyes, catching the copper light, fixed upon mine.

"Here she is," I said.

My guests followed my eyes and then looked back at me, frowning, grinning apologetically, eyebrows raised.

"Is she coming in?"

"No she's here. She doesn't come in. She's just here."

From their half-hearted, polite laughter I could tell that they thought that I was joking, but were unable to get the joke.

"She's…" I said. "But…" I held out my hand, and smiled. "Cornelia… let me introduce…"

And my guests began to leave. John and Daniel said they had to be somewhere, and slapped me heartily on the shoulder. Barney, looking pale, said that he'd travel back to town with the boys, and drank down his full glass of wine. Beverley and Fran lingered, but seemed unable to make conversation. They cast sympathetic smiles my way as they looked for their coats. I heard Daisy whisper "Perhaps we should stay?" but Lawrence shook his head.

Cornelia watched them, one by one, as they passed her on the way to the door. And, when we were left alone, she did

25

something that I'd never seen her do before.

Cornelia smiled.

Adjudicator's comments: When a story mentions the word 'ghost' in the first sentence you wonder if there are going to be any surprises, yet this piece is engaging and unusual from the start and all the way through. The author's style is direct and informal, occasionally using short, punchy sentences that keep you hooked. You might think the opening sentence 'I fell in love with a ghost' gives the whole game away, but the skill of the writer comes across as the reality of life mingles with this spooky element to make it all feel so possible. Some wonderful metaphors are used and the dialogue, when it arrives, is some of the most natural and well written of any of the stories in the competition. There are touches of humour throughout and the lovely ending leaves you longing for the unusual couple to find happiness together. To create characters you care about is always a sign of a good writer.

3rd Place

Panorama

By Alexander Sparrow

Alice was 17 when her mother died. She always called her that – mother – even though they weren't well off. It wasn't an affectation; Alice had none of those. We had just finished our last year at St Jude Girls' School. She'd always been quiet. Solitary. I thought someone would have been with her then, so soon after the death, but when I arrived at her home, she was alone. I'm not expecting you to believe the story she told me. You weren't there.

She was in her darkroom when I arrived, unpacking her equipment in the barely-there light, everything red in the glow of the coloured bulbs. There was barely any space, it was so full. She pulled out a pile of developed photos from a box. They were black and white. Then there was a large pair of scissors; several rolls of film; and a second stack of photos, smaller than the first. The walls were strung with clothesline and from them hung more photos. They were pegged by one corner, dripping into trays beneath. Her workspace was full, and there were larger prints stacked on the floor. The fumes were strong too. From the chemicals. You could barely breathe in there.

"Hi, Alice."

"Hi Sarah." She turned to look at me.

27

"It's hot in here," I said. "You must be suffocating." The room was packed to the brim, and I know it's the second or third time I've said that, but only repetition can emphasise how *full* that tiny room was. The smell of the chemicals singed the hairs in my nose; they reached in and burned them one by one. It made you feel faint even after only a minute or two. She didn't say any more. I told her it'd be good to clear some space, even if it meant boxing up some of the photos. "Get them out later if you want," I said. "But you need room for new memories."

That woke her up.

Alice stood there in her black dress. She only made this room work because she was small too. I was hunched over. She spoke quietly, like she always did.

"They'll always be there," she said.

"What will?"

"Memories. No matter what you do to forget them. I could take the photos and box them up, hide the boxes – *burn them*, if I wanted to. Wouldn't matter. Some things you don't forget."

She looked up at a line of photos. They were pegged haphazardly together, forming a panorama of an empty beach. I sat on a wooden stool in the corner as Alice continued. "My teacher said we should be inspired by what we've experienced. We should go back to our dreams and photograph those, or what we remember of them."

"How are you meant to do that?" I asked. "They're your *dreams*. They're not real."

She at looked at me for a moment before she turned the lights off and started working in the dark. The negative she was working on might have been another landscape. I couldn't make it out.

She began her story slowly. "It was a hot day. I would have been three or four. Maybe older, but I don't think so." She stopped there for a long time. I thought she was deciding

28

whether to continue. Maybe she was loading film.

It was best never to rush Alice.

"I was alone," she said, "digging in the sand. There weren't any people around. It was a hot day, but a workday – it must have been, otherwise the beach would have been full. The sun was hot. What I remember is me, alone in a hole, digging, and hot.

"I shouldn't have done it.

"If there were people swimming, they were in the water. Far from me. I was covered in sand. I thought if I could get deep enough, she wouldn't find me. Then I would win. So I tried to hide in the sand on an empty beach."

A red light brought the room out of darkness. There were more photos to hang. Many, *many* more. All at different stages of development. Rows of dripping prints circled us, lined every wall. She sat down opposite me. Looked me in the eye.

And slowly, slowly... images developed in the background.

What did she say before?

"She must have told me not to get dirty. She never liked me dirty... made her look bad. It wasn't winning I was thinking about. It was trying not to lose. I was scared when she arrived. I wanted to jump out of my clothes, out of my *skin* – anything to be clean again. I remember her eyes were small and blue and harsh. They were broken and dead. She wasn't happy with my sandy shoes. Hair full of sand, my face and arms and legs gritty with the stuff. And I remember it was *hot*.

"Mother was so *angry*... but soon I was having fun again."

We should be inspired by what we've experienced.

I remember Alice was shaking.

"I was still sitting in the hole, legs covered in sand, and she joined me. She'd never done that before. Her eyes came to life. She was even smiling. She helped me dig deeper and deeper and I went from sitting to standing. I pushed down the sand around my feet – mother showed me how – and I pressed each

29

layer as hard as I could. She looked almost proud.

"The sand came to my waist and I couldn't move my legs. We made a good team.

"She started pushing the sand in herself now, back into the hole. I kept my arms still. She'd told me to leave them by my sides. The closer the sand got to the surface, the hotter it was. My feet were cool, but I was only up to my elbows and if I'd moved, I could have got out.

"It was so hot when it got to my shoulders, I almost said something, but she'd never played with me before and I could see from the smile on her face she was having fun. I didn't want it to stop.

"It would have made a great photo, but I didn't have a camera then. I was too young. Too young to dig properly, let alone take a good picture. She was burying me in the sand, right up to my neck.

"The sand got too hot for me. You couldn't even walk barefoot on it. I couldn't move to turn my head. And it was over my chin and tickling the bottom of my ears.

"Mother had stopped smiling.

"I tried to say something but I couldn't." Alice shook her head. "I *couldn't*," she said again, to herself this time.

The darkroom, full with equipment, chemicals, and two bodies had been stifling before. Now I was cold.

"Things go vague then. Hazy," she said.

Alice looked me straight in the face with those blue, watery eyes. "I sometimes think she buried me too deep... until I was completely under the sand." She stood up then, bumping a pile of black and white photos off the desk. There must have been more than a hundred of them.

I heard again her words: *inspired by what we experience*. She didn't notice the photos fall. There were prints lining the walls, covering the floor. Everywhere. I only noticed then what the photos showed.

"It ends there… in darkness. And heat."

It was best never to rush Alice. When I put my hand on her shoulder, she gently shrugged it off.

"I don't expect you to believe me. You weren't there." She turned the red light on full.

The photos had developed. I left her there, where I found her: surrounded by thousands of dripping and hanging and piled and fallen photos of the beach.

Adjudicators Comments: Although this story didn't have the same obviously spooky elements as many of the other submissions, it was certainly one of the most eerie tales, which I found myself reading several times over. Although, at around 1,300 words, this was one of the shortest pieces in the whole competition, it certainly didn't detract from the depth of the story. Unusually the narrator was not the one who suffered spooky goings on this time, but it was her role to extract the story from the main character – a troubled girl who had clearly been through some sort of trauma. The writer's great skill showed as the girl slowly explained what had happened to her, in a way that left me with a growing dread inside. The end was not neatly tied up, as is the case in most stories, but left me wondering of possible implications. This could have been unsatisfying and annoying but somehow wasn't and left me thinking about the story long after I had read it. I would love to read more from this memorable writer.

SHORTLISTED

A Flash of White

by Rebecca Burton

Barry glanced up at the steep Fell that gradually filled the windscreen of his car as he wove through the country lanes. It loomed over the Eden Valley, glowing green and gold under the weak wintry sun as it eclipsed the horizon in front of him.

Parking in the village of Blencarn near the path to the summit, he climbed out of the car and gathered his day-pack. Food, water, maps, mobile, whistle, emergency bivvy bag, thermos - everything he might need for the walk. He stamped his feet a few times to settle them into his hiking boots and locked the car.

His son, Jonathan, stood beside him, dressed in jeans and a t-shirt. Smudges of dirt covered his face and arms, and a brown stain clung to his knee. Twenty-five years old, and he was still the same scruffy little boy.

"Come on then, lad. Better get cracking. That mountain won't climb itself."

Jonny smiled and followed Barry through the gate, onto the path that lead to the Fell's flank.

Neither spoke as they crossed the first pasture and navigated thickets of broom. The last week had seen heavy rain and the grass squelched underfoot as they walked. Barry was glad of his boots and gaiters that kept his feet dry in the long grass, especially when they reached Littledale Beck, which raced with the weight of the additional water.

They forded the stream and began to climb. Barry's eyes fell to his muddy boots as he pulled himself up the incline and then, from the corner of his eye, a white flash. And again. Jonny's bright white trainers kept pace beside him. "I don't

33

know how you keep your shoes so clean in this muck. Still, you should have worn boots. You'll miss them when we hit the scree."

Jonny just smiled his inscrutable smile. The damn boy was headstrong. Always followed his own path and consequences be damned.

He should have brought his son here years ago, Barry thought, like his father had brought him, linking those who had come before with those who would come after. Until the family line ran out, at any rate.

Together, he and Jonny had climbed Snowdon and Ben Nevis. They'd conquered the Yorkshire Three Peaks and trekked in the Brecon Beacons, but they'd never made it up here, to the top of Great Dun Fell. Not until today.

They'd tried the climb once when the boy was about seven, but the weather had been too bad that day. He shouldn't have left it so long to try again. The Fell was just too close to home maybe. It was always easier to travel to find adventure than look for it on your doorstep.

The boy had certainly done his fair share of adventuring. Always off with his friends –Thailand, the Himalayas, South America. If he wasn't riding his motorbike, he was jumping out of a plane. Or scuba-diving, or pot-holing. Always something new and always something dangerous. Barry worried the whole time he was away and yet people were killed every day just crossing the road. You never knew what was around the next bend.

In his more honest moments, Barry had to admit that he had been a little jealous of Jonny's adventures. It was a different world for the young. But the two of them had the hills, and that was all that really mattered.

They crested the rise and the path flattened out, although steep slopes of scree still hung over them as they strode on.

Barry caught his breath again. "Lad, did I ever tell you

about the Helm Wind? It's fascinating stuff."

Jonny nodded, a wry grin on his face. Of course, Barry had told him. Not just once, but many times. It was a shared story from Jonny's childhood, part of the family lore; a well-worn tale of the Helm Wind and of Grandpa Joe, Barry's dad, and how he had taken Barry up Great Dun Fell to see the huge Helm Cloud that gave the wind its name.

"See how the sky is clear above us, lad? That's because of the wind. It blows from the northeast and falls from the edge of the fells. It rushes down into the valley and as the air cools, it leaves that great cloud up on top of the Fell, there." Barry pointed up at the mass of silvery cloud that boiled over the top of the mountain. From the path they were climbing, the peak of the Fell was lost in the darkness that glowered above the scree.

"Someone thought it looked a bit like a helmet and that gives the wind its name. The cold wind rushes down the side of the fell and hits the warm air of the valley, which forces it back up and creates another cloud, the Helm Bar, which spreads out to cover the whole valley. So, you get this one clear bit left in the middle, even today when the northeaster isn't so strong. Imagine what it must be like when the wind blows full force! That must be something, eh?"

Talking distracted him from the effort of climbing until they finally breached the belt of scree that encircled the summit. As they walked closer, the great cloud seemed to lift ahead of them and hung like a ceiling above the plateau that ran across the shoulder of the three neighbouring fells.

A cairn marked the edge of the plateau. "Good place for a sit down and a spot of lunch, eh, lad?"

Barry eased down with a groan to lean against the cairn as Jonny plonked himself on the ground beside him.

Barry dug his sarnies out of his bag and munched for a few minutes. "I'm right glad there's no proper Helm Wind today.

Up to 60 miles an hour, they say, on a bad day. A man can barely stand in that. Your Grandpa Joe told me stories of men being blown right off their horses." He paused for another bite. "Must get right cold up here. You doing alright in that t-shirt?"

Jonny nodded.

"If we had more time, we could follow the Pennine Way across the summit of Cross Fell over yonder, and take the old corpse road back down to the valley. Can you imagine it, having to carry the dead miles over the moor to the nearest churchyard for burial?" Barry shuddered. "Brrr. Makes the blood run cold. Though it's a grand path to walk, mind, if you're not bothered by spooks. Another time, mayhap."

He finished his sandwiches and put the wrappings back into his rucksack. "Best be getting on. Few more miles to get under our feet yet."

They walked on together until they stood at the edge of the scarp, the valley spread out under their feet. It looked like a model train set all laid out for them to play with, Barry thought.

"There," he said, pointing. "That must be Skirwith. That's where Grandpa Joe grew up. He spent hours up on these hills as a boy. He told me he even met a man who studied the weather up here, back before the war. Must have been a bit mad, staying up here in the winter in the snows. But he's the one that discovered how the wind works."

Silence fell between them again. It was the full, heavy kind of silence that knows something is coming. The kind of silence that spreads just before a thunderstorm or a solar eclipse. A pregnant silence. The weight of it hung around Barry's neck and bowed his head.

"I should stop delaying matters and do what I came here to do, I suppose," Barry said at last. He turned to his son and allowed his gaze to linger on the boy's face. "I haven't said this enough but I love you, lad. I hope you know that."

Jonny smiled, his eyes shining. Barry could now see that the smudges on his face and arms were cuts and bruises, and the stain on his jeans had shifted hues to become the dirty red of dried blood.

Barry pulled the thermos out of his bag. With infinite care he tipped the contents out to fall down the side of the scarp until the cloud of ash was caught by the wind and whipped into the sky.

Alone, he carried on watching long after the last traces had disappeared, until the tears had dried cold on his face.

For just a moment, the wind dropped and the absence of it glowed warm on Barry's skin. "Take care of him for me Da," he whispered into the still air. "Until I can come join you both." Then, the calm was over and the wind blew on, as strong as ever.

Barry shook himself, scrubbing at his cheeks with the back of one hand. With a sigh, he replaced the thermos in his bag, then glanced at his watch. Two-thirty, and it would take another couple of hours to get back yet. His Mary would be waiting and worrying. Time to go home.

Adjudicator's feedback: Well written and engaging, this was one of those stories that has a twist at the end that seems obvious once you get there, but certainly had me guessing throughout. I felt a fondness for the protagonist, Barry, from the start, which helped build the tension very slowly as I gradually realised something was amiss. The gentle dialogue worked well, Barry's Northern accent quickly becoming apparent, and it was cleverly handled so that the one-sided nature of it was not obvious to begin with.

Anniversary

Louise Wilford

The temperature drops as we make our way home over the moors.

It had been a lovely anniversary - we'd walked round Nelly Moss lakes at Cragside (where Mark proposed to me ten years ago), crunching through leaves and pine cones, greeting other walkers and stroking their dogs, breathing in lungfuls of cool Autumn air with a hint of wood smoke from the small fires the gardeners had lit to burn the bracken they were clearing. Mark is, of course, a serious hiker – he'd done the Three Peaks in Snowdonia and walked the whole of the Transpennine Trail. I'm more of a casual rambler, but it was nice to walk together for once, even though for Mark this was only a gentle stroll.

I'd even gathered a few handfuls of late bilberries, the shiny berries gleaming like mouse-eyes from a patch growing beside a small waterfall, as we walked through the woods back to our car. Mark loved bilberries, and I could use them to develop a new recipe for the latest book, if I could ever get back to it. Phyllida, my agent, had been nagging me again. Maybe I could take the North-East of England as my theme – Tyneside Singin' Hinny and the like. Food made from local produce. I wondered if you could dry bilberries and what they'd be like, and felt a brief stirring of enthusiasm, like a small bird fluttering its wings in the pit of my brain, but it quickly subsided, as it always did these days. Phyllida would just have to keep on nagging.

In the afternoon, we stopped for lunch at a pub in Rothbury, the stone wall at the front guarded by a row of pumpkin jack-o-lanterns which flickered oddly as we passed them.

The man behind the bar told us they'd had a pumpkin-carving competition for the local children. I smiled at him, remembering the pumpkins that we'd seen that weekend Mark proposed, adorning doorways and shopfronts, simultaneously jolly and freakish.

The barman recognised me from my cookery show and said I could take one of the pumpkins if I liked. 'Maybe you could do a pumpkin recipe and mention us in your next book,' he suggested. I smiled at him and said I'd certainly think about it, but I knew I wouldn't. Somehow, I just can't focus on cooking these days. If I'm honest, I haven't been able to focus on anything for months, not since...well, not since it happened.

We set off home as the evening drifted in, our new carved pumpkin, unlit now of course, sitting on the parcel-shelf of the Audi like a weird Halloween satnav. The moors had been glowing with orange light on our way west, but now the evening sky is darkening a little. White streamers of mist are gathering in the valleys, drifting into the roadside undergrowth. And on the hilltops, the moorland spreads out on every side like a gnarly duvet thrown over midnight sleepers.

'It's still gorgeous, isn't it?' I say, glancing sideways at him from the driver's seat. He's looking out over the moors and doesn't respond. He's always been a quiet man; it's what I first loved about him. He looks out over a landscape as if he's breathing it all in, making it a part of himself. The moors, of course, have a special place in his heart. He was brought up in Alnmouth and he walked here often as a young man. He knows these moors like he knows his own skin. I'd probably never have come up here if it wasn't for him. I'm a Londoner from my Charles Worthington bob to my Selfridges sandals.

There are no other cars on the road. In front of us, I can see it stretching ahead, a pale ribbon dipping and rising, and through the rear-view mirror it stretches backwards, vanishing into the darkness. I can also see the carved pumpkin grinning toothily at me, and for a second I feel suddenly cold. I turn up the car's heater a little.

'We'll be back in Alnwick in twenty minutes,' I say, half sad, half relieved. I'm tired, if truth be known. Exhausted. I've probably done more exercise today than I've done all year. I can't seem to get myself motivated. I seem to spend my days sitting round the house, waiting for Mark to get home so we can curl up together on the settee and watch our favourite box sets. I've done no work on the cookery book I'm supposed to be writing – it's still just six and a half recipes, the same as it was before. To be honest, I don't really cook anymore, even for myself. I often forget to eat these days, and more often than not I just open a can of soup or take a ready-meal out of the freezer. My readers would freak if they knew! Phyllida was understanding at first but she's been quite irritated by me missing deadlines lately, says I'll be lucky to have the book published by the Christmas after next by which time people might have forgotten I exist. *You have to strike while the iron's hot in this business*, she says. Well, at least I've got those bilberries now – I'll make Mark's favourite bilberry and almond cake when we get home. I try to include his favourite recipes in the book when I can. Maybe I *should* do a pumpkin recipe?

I glance back at the ghoulish face on the parcel shelf and grimace.

I wasn't sure about this anniversary trip north, if I'm honest. I wondered whether it might be too much for me. But I am glad we did it. It was a real pleasure. I hadn't been to Cragside since he proposed, all those years ago, and it was great to visit it again. *He'd* been up here lots of times since, of course, hiking with his friends and sometimes alone, while I was busy filming my new TV series or working on my latest book. London is so far from Northumberland and I know he misses the countryside – Greenwich Park is nice but it isn't really a substitute for the moors! But he never complains. He knows my work means I have to be in London, and he's always been happy to support me as long as he can go on his hikes now and then. 'Recharging' is what he calls it.

Looking at his profile now, I can see how these hills have shaped him. His skin is browner, more weather-beaten than mine, his hair just beginning to turn grey – I think it makes him look interesting, along with his pale blue eyes and the lines round them from squinting in all weathers. He's always been an attractive man. I've seen other women glancing admiringly at him, but I know he'd never leave me. Seeing him beside me in the car provokes a sudden need to kiss him, tell him how I feel about him. But he seems so self-possessed, so wrapped in his own thoughts, that I don't feel I can disturb him. Anyway, I'm driving.

We're at the brow of a hill when it happens. Suddenly, I see a flicker of yellowish light in the mirror, like a distant flame, and the murky interior of the car becomes suddenly brighter. For a moment, I think that a car has come up behind us, headlights on full beam, but where could it have come from? A moment earlier there were no cars behind or in front.

I glance over my shoulder and the Audi swerves into the edge of the road as I slam on the brakes in shock.

'Christ almighty!'

The pumpkin face is now lit up by a candle flame that has suddenly, inexplicably, re-ignited.

The car judders to a halt, the anti-lock brakes kicking in, one wheel on the mossy, muddy verge. We both turn round to look at the pumpkin. It must be a prank, of course, a joke pumpkin – some sort of mechanism inside to make it light up at random moments. The barman must have let us have it as some sort of Trick or Treat nonsense. Very funny, I think, though I'm not amused. He might have caused a car accident, or a fire.

The pumpkin continues to glow eerily, light spilling from

41

a jagged mouth and frowning eye-holes that seem now somehow more devilish, less charming, than they seemed earlier.

I realise Mark's no longer in the passenger seat. He's somehow got out of the car, though I didn't hear the door opening, and he's standing on the edge of the moorland staring out, away from me. The bag of bilberries has spilled across the seat.

Suddenly, I'm angry. What's he doing, leaving me to deal with this while he arses about staring dreamily across the landscape like some sort of cut-price Heathcliff? I open the driver's door, clamber out of the car, my legs stiff, and open the rear door, sticking in my head so I can blow out the flame in the pumpkin before it sets my bloody car on fire. It's giving off more heat than I expected and I can't get close enough to see whether it's a conventional candle or not, but I blow at it anyway, with little effect. The flame simply flickers and then grows bigger, like those joke candles people put on birthday cakes. The grinning face laughs silently at me.

Shaken, I back out of the car and run round to Mark. He's still standing there, his hands in his trouser pockets in that familiar stance. Why is he doing this to me?

He turns and smiles that sweet old smile he always used to give me before he left on one of his hikes. He'd hoist up his backpack, then smile down at me, wistful and kind, as if he wished I could go with him but knew I wasn't ready yet. I can see the ghostly outline of a backpack on his shoulders now.

Then he steps forward onto the brown heather, pulling a bilberry from his pocket and popping it in his mouth as he always used to do, and strides onto the moor towards the place where he died – alone – last year, of a heart attack.

Behind me in the car, the pumpkin's flame winks out. I lean against the passenger door, defeated, watching my husband stride away across the moors.

Adjudicators feedback: The chatty, relaxed, style of the narration of this piece quickly drew me in and gave me a false sense of security – silly when you're reading a spooky story! I came to care about the narrator so the ending was sad and tragic and unexpected all at the same time, cleverly hidden by a few red herrings along the way. So well written I could certainly imagine reading a much longer story by this writer.

Cover-Up

Louise Goulding

Nick has kind eyes and a dirty laugh. He suggests a relaxed, quirky little bar that serves food until late, and he orders olives and leans across the table to help himself to my sweet potato fries. We talk about the books that once set our teenage selves on fire, and the music that made us wrap our arms around our mates' shoulders and sing along.

It's all so easy. Nick tells stories that make me belly-laugh, and we talk as though we've known each other for years – talk until the bar is empty. He has a speck of something herby in his teeth, but I kiss him anyway, in the taxi that drops us both off at my door; offering him coffee that I don't make until the next morning.

He has tattoos. The piece across his chest is fascinating and beautiful. At first glance, while he's sitting propped against the pillows, it looks like a geometric jangle of triangles. But closer, slower – fingertips tracing, back under the bed sheets – I realise it's a fleet of paper aeroplanes.

"It's lovely," I tell him.

On his thigh is a panther, climbing. Its tail coils down to his knee, front paws digging ink-red claw marks towards his groin. The panther is black, with a sleek blue highlight along its spine. Its head is turned sideways in profile, showing bulging yellow eyes and a red mouth.

"It's a cover-up," Nick says, "I had to pick a design off the guy's wall chart, but he said it had to be something with a lot of black ink. It was this or an 8 ball." Faintly, as the morning sun hits it, I can almost make out the shapes of the old design within the panther's body. Classic 90s tribal, perhaps? He'd be about the right age.

Nick leans forward, turns to put his empty cup on my bed-side table. On the back of his shoulder is a faded assortment of Chinese symbols.

"Family, courage, honour, peace," he explains, smiling. "You know – all the stuff that's actually meaningful to every-body, so there's no need to get it tattooed. But we all do these things when we're 18 and we think we're being profound."

I laugh, and show him the decade-old butterfly that was my earnest attempt at a flash of identity on my hip, as soon as I had ID.

"I keep thinking about getting it covered up," Nick says, rubbing a hand towards his Chinese characters, "but I haven't found anything I want yet. Plus it helps that I don't ever see it."

"I think you should keep it," I tell him. "It's like a passport stamp – it's who you were then." He grins, and when he kisses me on the forehead I can still feel the smile. So we spend our first Sunday together with kisses and coffee, and a walk to the corner café for toasted sandwiches as it starts to get dark.

Nick has a nice flat and a ginger cat called Slim. She rubs against my ankles, rumbling loudly, leaving fur on my jeans while Nick makes risotto. He stirs the rice and I pour us each a glass of wine and flick through his MP3 player, make a little playlist. We laugh and dance, and the risotto sticks to the pan.

It starts with a papercut.

I'm in the shower one morning when I find it: a tiny line on one fingertip that stings when I rub in my shampoo. I frown at it – I don't remember doing it at work yesterday – but it's just a little thing, and Nick is making breakfast.

The next week there are more little things, hovering on the edges of explainable. A scrape appears on my heel, but it could have been my shoe rubbing. A bruise on my ribs, small and dark as a blackberry. A tender patch on the back of my head; Nick gently parts my hair and confirms there's a little

45

red mark.

Then the dreams begin. Not every night, but often enough that I start to feel uneasy about falling asleep. The dreams are dark – no sight, just sensation. They are all panic and chase, blindly pelting down alleys, pursued. I jolt myself awake with an ache in my chest, my legs tight, sickly-hot. But Nick is there, curling an arm around me, soft until the sweating stops.

"It's ok," he strokes my hair, "I'm here, and you're ok. It's ok. It's all ok."

Our weekends are sweet and warm. Nick is good music and bad scrambled eggs; he is evening walks and late-night conversations. We curl ourselves in and hibernate, with the cat and a boxset and my amazing homemade nachos, delivered with a smug flourish. Nick eats all the jalapenos and I begin to leave a toothbrush at his flat.

The dreams get blacker, louder. There are noises in the dark – a low, menacing rumble and the constant ragged sound of something breathing. Or maybe that's me? I run. I run through the dark until my lungs burn, urging my legs on as they grow wobbly. I wake up with another new bruise, small and dark on my neck, like a lovebite.

Finally, one night, it breaks cover. In the dark of the dream there's a slick glint of blue, coiling around to face me. Sharp white teeth in a red mouth, and bulging yellow eyes. I whimper through the lump in my throat, and the panther snarls. I wake with a shriek, leap out of Nick's arms as he tries to hold me, clambering away from him across the room.

"It's you!" I point, flapping my hands to swat him away. My mind races. "You! You and that thing!"

He's awake and asking questions. He doesn't understand. He's pulling on a pair of shorts, telling me not to be crazy, but I'm out in the street and running to my car. There's a long red scrape down my forearm. It's been Nick all along. I need to get home.

For days, I ignore his calls. I leave for work 20 minutes early and take the long way home, just in case he tries to stop me. The bruise on my neck isn't healing in the normal brown and yellow way, it's getting darker. I wear a scarf in the office. I message Kelly Gallagher's brother and ask him for something to help me sleep. My salvation is instant and dreamless, with the stiffest tension headaches in the mornings.

I call in sick, spend a day watching boxsets and planning to clear out my wardrobe, just as soon as I can find the energy to move. Maybe tomorrow I'll get a haircut. My mind donates most of my clothes to the charity shop and rearranges some furniture. My body sits on the sofa, eating crisps.

Nick texts.

Please talk to me. I don't understand. I don't know what happened and I miss you. Please.

Having to talk it through again feels worse than the situation itself. But I want him gone.

Psycho, I'm onto you. I get it now. You were hurting me when I was asleep.

He calls and I don't answer.

What?? God, no. No. I would never hurt you, I swear. I would never.

I don't know why you did it. But that just proves I'm a good person, Nick, because I CANNOT imagine why you'd do this. But I know it was you. I didn't want to believe it, so high on lust and denial, my brain made me dream it was your tattoo.

What??

Your stupid, naff retro panther.

There's a long pause. Good, ok, we're done. What else could he say? I leave my phone on the side, go and pour a glass of wine, turn on the tv in my bedroom and sit wrapped in the duvet, still in my jeans. My head aches - full of a thick mix of exhaustion and dark thoughts. I suppose I should report this. I assume the police will take a note of domestic violence, even if I slept through it and can't remember the actual details. My scratches and marks will help. The thought of having to show them to a police officer makes me feel sick. I get up and look in the mirror.

The bruise on my neck is… different. It's a tiny pawprint.

I'm leaning into the mirror, staring in disbelief, so when my phone pings it makes me jump and frighten myself with the face I pull. When I pick it up, I see it's actually the third unread message.

No. No, please. Don't joke about this.
Not again. This can't be happening again. Are you serious?
If you're serious about this, you are in real danger.

I stare at my phone, scared of every possibility of this, whatever the hell this is. Frantically rubbing the bruise on my neck with the other hand. I drain the wineglass, pour another. A new bottle, another glass. I pace the kitchen, knock over a lamp, and finally fall asleep fully clothed, sideways across the end of the bed.

The panther is waiting. Yellow eyes and white claws in the dark. I try to run, but my legs are too warm, too soft with the wine. I stumble and fall against a wall, heaving breaths. No, not a wall – it's a tree. The panther curls out from behind the trunk, black skin, red mouth and those bright teeth.

"No!" I tell it, feebly. Too sad, too drunk to fight. My knees crumple and I grip the tree. But the panther is limping. Bleeding. One front paw is a bloody stump. One ear is torn and its face and back are carved with lines of gore. It snarls, blood dripping from its teeth.

"No!" I scream at it, aiming a kick at its one good eye. It shrieks, and the whole world spins as my legs give out, and I fall as the panther is shrieking – or maybe it's me – and I jolt awake at the end of my bed.

My mouth is so dry that I gag when I try to swallow. My throat burns like screaming. My phone says 2:46am. 2 missed calls. 1 message, an hour ago:

Help.

Nick is sleeping, but the doctor walks me to a side room anyway. She has questions – did Nick have a history of self-harm? I tell her no, not that I knew of, but as I bite dents into my third empty polystyrene cup and watch the rhythm of his sedated breathing, I wonder again whether I really knew Nick at all.

A cheesegrater. There were marks from a knife, she explains, but it's really hard to do that to yourself. I feel the hospital coffee rise in my throat as I contemplate how a cheesegrater would possibly be any easier, but that's what they say he did. I think of the gore-lines streaking the panther's back.

A nurse says I can't stay. I'm not even sure I would want to. I stroke Nick's hair, sweat-curled at the temples, and kiss his forehead. He stirs, blinks thickly, and smiles when he sees me. Then he's awake. Urgent.

"They won't cut it off!" he tells me desperately. The nurse comes in, tells Nick to calm down, lie down. He's elbowing the pillow to sit up, to find eye contact with me.

"I tried! I tried so hard, but it won't work. It won't stop it!" Nick is shouting, and I'm already walking as the nurse tells me to leave.

Nick's voice is high, clamouring, as I make it to the ward door.

"They need to just take my whole leg off, but they won't! I asked them, but they won't take it!"

Adjudicator's feedback: This intriguing tale has so much detail it's hard to believe it's all fiction – a sign of a great imagination. Everything is very realistic and going well for the narrator for the first quarter of the story, and when things start to go wrong it's introduced so gently you can't tell where the piece is heading. The ending when it comes is both unexpected and shocking. A wonderfully unusual read.

Forgiveness

Lesley Bowen

She was sitting alone by the seafront when I first spotted her. She stood out because the sky was the shade of grey that people hurry beneath rather than settle under. I didn't know who she was of course at that stage but something drew me to her. Perhaps it was the way she was hunched over with her arm wrapped around her knees, her head dipped downwards; the only reason I could think that anyone would be bearing the full frontal of the North Sea wind was if they were admiring the tumbling waves in front of them. But she wasn't.

Sammy was scampering around my feet for his ball so I threw it again but this time in the direction of the lady; I didn't like the thought of waking up tomorrow to a local news story about a young woman drowning herself in the sea and knowing that a simple display of manners on my part might have prevented it.

Sammy lurched away towards the ball, which had fallen within metres of the lady, but she didn't seem to notice. The only movement was the writhing of her hair in the wind. Sammy was making a dash for the sea now and, whilst I didn't particularly want a soggy dog to take home, it did enable me to get closer. I decided I would stroll down to where the waves clawed at the sand, summon Sammy then, as I turned back, take the opportunity to ask the lady if she was okay. If she didn't move soon the tide would be clambering over her feet.

"Sammy," I called. "Sammy, come on."

I patted my legs and he bounded out of the sea, then I took the few steps required to be within earshot.

"Excuse me, are you okay?"

She looked up, our eyes met and I took a sharp breath inwards.

"Hello Kelly," she said.

I needed to find a way to focus through the history, now seizing my body and giving it a brutal shake but Sammy was back, waiting for the ball. I threw it, hard this time and, when he had scurried after it, I looked back at Teresa. Years of shame were fighting their way up my gullet and trying to escape, to release the pressure I had been retaining for more than twenty years. I tried to speak but there were too many words trying to come out at once so that in the end none of them could.

Teresa was watching me, neither smiling nor stern. She patted the sand beside her, never taking her eyes from my face. I looked for Sammy, he was entertaining himself with the ball a little further along the seafront. I walked across and sat down close to the spot where Teresa had indicated. Being scrutinised in this way by someone who had last seen me as barely more than a child was an uncomfortable feeling, as though sharing our childhood could enable her to see further inside than most. If only that was a skill I possessed back then; maybe I would have seen the pain we'd caused her sooner and stopped before things became irreversible.

The silence was becoming tense and I decided to break it with the most obvious words I could summon.

"I'm sorry."

"I can't tell whether you mean it because you're not looking at me when you say it."

It seemed such a peculiar thing to respond with. I had expected a rant about sorry not being sufficient to atone for the upset I had caused her, so I waited for her to continue, but she didn't and when I looked into her face I could feel my cheeks burn from her gaze. Her eyes were not how I remembered: bluer, more beautiful, less haunted. They invited, no, encouraged me to say more. So I did.

"I often ask myself why. Why did I treat you that way? And I don't have an answer, which makes it worse."

I waited for a reaction but none came so I carried on.

"When I wake up my first feeling is guilt, not necessarily a conscious sense of it but an undertone that is the starting point, every day."

Another pause followed and I breathed into it before a sense of urgency nudged me along.

"I don't see them anymore you know, Emma or Marie. Haven't spoken to them since we left. I did try to find you though, on Friends Reunited and Facebook, figured even a cowardly apology was better than none at all."

I felt a hand on my arm then and, as if it had squeezed them from me, tears began to trickle from my eyes. I could taste salt but wasn't sure whether it came from my crying or the sea air.

"Well you've found me now," she said and we sat like that for a while, me wiping tears from my face whilst she rubbed my arm. Sammy, bored of occupying himself, returned with the ball and dropped it at Teresa's feet. She laughed, a sound I didn't think I had ever heard from her before, then picked up the ball and threw it.

"He won't leave you alone now," I said.

"I always wanted a dog," she said. "He's very sweet."

We must have sat on that beach for an hour in the end: talking, sitting in silence then talking again. It wasn't until I felt the first drops hit my head, saw the splashes on my arms, that I remembered the colour of the clouds when I first observed Teresa and thought how lucky it was that the rain had held off for so long. In a moment of boldness, I spoke again.

"Do you want to get a coffee somewhere?"

She turned so her body was facing mine and it struck me then how young she looked.

"I have to go now Kelly but I want you to know that I forgive you for everything. You've been punishing yourself for too long, I can see that in your eyes. It's time to move on, to live as the good adult you've become, not the teenager that you used to be."

She leaned towards me and pulled me to her in an embrace, held me there for a minute, then stood. I followed her lead and pulled my hood up.

Her presence was so calming that I didn't want her to leave. I watched her walking along the beach until the rain became heavy, then I yelled to Sammy and hurried to find shelter. I turned again when we reached the promenade but she had gone.

Over the course of the following weeks I relaxed into myself in a way that I never had before. The feeling of living in a fog, of not properly being able to feel emotions, lifted. I found myself being surprised by all the different shades of green in a tree canopy or moved by stories on the news in a way that I hadn't experienced for a long time. I decided I'd spent too much time alone, wallowing in the shadow of my teenage self and that I would make an effort to get out more, socialise, make new friends.

What I really wanted though was to see Teresa again. She had such a reassuring aura that I wondered why I had never noticed it at school. Perhaps I had, perhaps that was the problem. I thought back to our conversation on the beach, when I referred to Facebook. She hadn't said whether or not she was on it; it was worth a look. I searched her name but soon realised it was a futile effort; had she been wearing a wedding ring? Next I looked for a Teresa amongst friends of old school friends; something I had avoided until now, having made the decision to divorce my past a long time ago. I went to the kitchen, poured a small glass of merlot then returned to my laptop and began to type in all the names I could remember. I left Emma and Marie until last but when their faces appeared on my screen they just looked ordinary, like any middle aged woman you would pass on the street. I don't know what else I expected. Still there was no Teresa but I found myself scrolling through other people's photos of the scenery that I had withdrawn myself from so long ago and yearning to be in those patches of sunlight on the mountainside. I made a decision.

I was out walking again, this time along a Scottish harbour, watching boats bobbing on the sun dressed sea and trying not to be allured by the smell of frying fish and vinegar soaked chips, when I saw another familiar face from the past. Sarah had been a couple of years above me at school but we lived on the same housing estate so always acknowledged each other, shared the walk home on a couple of occasions. The old me would have turned and walked in the opposite direction but instead I approached. She looked up and I watched her face for a trace of recognition. It came immediately.

"Oh my God, I remember you," she said. "Give me a minute, Kathy, no Kelly."

I laughed and we shook hands.

"Strange that we've not bumped into each other before."

"Not really. I moved to Norfolk about twenty years ago, just visiting. Although, funnily enough, I bumped into someone else from school there last week."

"Did you move for work?"

"No, fancied trying somewhere else, loved it and never came back."

The words dried up then and I realised that we'd not really shared our past, just encountered each other in it on occasion. I was about to say my farewells when she spoke again.

"Who was it?"

"Who?"

"The person you saw from school."

"Oh, it was Teresa Jennings." Sarah was frowning, trying to recall her I supposed. "She was in my year, you might not have know her."

She narrowed her eyes.

"Were you good friends?"

I hesitated, assessed how truthful to be. "Not really, just in the same class."

"It couldn't have been Teresa."

"Why not?"

"She died."

We must have been thinking about different people.

"There was another Teresa in the year below me, do you mean her?"

"No, it was definitely Teresa Jennings, not a name I'd forget. It was in the newspapers at the time. Tragic."

I stared at the lady in front of me. Was she who I thought she was? Was I who she thought I was? It felt like my brain was a spinning top and every time it started to slow, and I could focus, someone picked it up and twisted it fast.

"In the newspapers? What happened?"

"Hung herself the year we left school. Never left a letter or anything but her parents blamed it on bullying, said it'd gone on all through high school."

I heard a voice calling the name Sarah, watched her turn away towards a man gesturing a take-away coffee cup to her, then back to me, saw her mouth move but couldn't hear the words then she was walking away, my sanity trailing along behind her.

Sometimes I think about travelling back up to Scotland, visiting Teresa's grave, taking flowers, some yellow ones, maybe roses with some white freesias mixed in. But then I walk down to the spot where we sat on that steely day and I can feel forgiveness in the breeze, hear it in the exhalation of the waves. If I close my eyes I'm sure I can feel a tenderness brushing my arm. I expect some of the other dog walkers think I'm mad but none of them ever approach me, as I did Teresa. Maybe I am mad but, whatever I did or didn't see that day, I haven't felt haunted since.

Adjudicator's feedback: An evocative and endearing story with a touch of melancholy throughout. Although the surprise conclusion was the same as quite a few other spooky stories in this collection that didn't detract from the emotion it produced. And it didn't end quite there – the author providing a satisfying end to the tale that gave it so much more realism you could easily forget it was spooky fiction. This helped it stand out from others where the surprise ending is sudden and leaves the reader hanging.

Guising and Souling

Cathy Rushworth

"Bride of Dracula-tick. Two skeletons- tick, tick. One banshee, three ghosts in various sizes, one werewolf and a …a…? Casey-May Mathews, what exactly are you?"

"I'm half alien, half superhero, Miss. My mam didn't have time to go supermarket for a new outfit."

"Mmmm, not sure if it's quite the outfit I'd have chosen for trick or treating. But then if it was left to me I wouldn't be doing this at all."

"Sorry Miss. My mam said it'd have to do."

"Well then, it'll have to do, won't it? Right you lot get your containers and pumpkins and let's go. Now I'm going to let you all have a tea light for your pumpkins but *I'm* going to light them outside and remember they can be dangerous so no messing about. Jacob please put Benjamin down.

Remember we don't really want to scare anyone, especially not any elderly people. Just think on- you've all heard what happened when Kyle Lewis dressed up as the Grim Reaper and jumped out at Mr Robertson. Old Mr Robertson with the dicky heart, rest his soul."

Mrs Collins led the youth group at the local church hall, a multi-functional seventies delight of a building with asbestos ceiling and cheap cladding on the outside, and on the inside bare magnolia walls which needed a repaint and cheap plastic chairs and tables. Big cork noticeboards with leaflets advertised a variety of events from toddler groups to weightwatchers, model train clubs to flower arranging. Any way to get people in.

Mrs Collins managed to get the children into some sort of

group and led them out of the youth club. This was her least favourite event of the year, not really agreeing with Hallowe'en and the Americanised trick or treating. But even she couldn't help smiling when she saw the obvious delight of the children when their pumpkins came alive with the glow of a small flame.

"Jacob, this is the third and last time I light yours. It will keep going out if you insist on trying to pick up Benjamin.

Trick or treating is bullying really, she thought. *Demanding treats with menaces.*

But *she* wasn't in charge and the powers that be (in their wisdom) thought it was a good way for the children 'to interact with their community and create bonds within the safe environment of the youth group.'

"Hmmmm," was her response to that.

The chill October night sent shivers down the spine and Mrs Collins pulled her sensible fleecy coat tighter. Those kids must be freezing in their flimsy outfits. Kids don't seem to feel the cold though. They made their way round the local streets. The shadows of the trees stood out black against the grey shades of the night sky. The moon wasn't quite full, but nearly. Wisps of cloud obscured it, dulling it to a faint glow. A spattering of stars tried to shine brightly but again the clouds gave them a muted effect. Bright orange pumpkins gleamed evil menace through cutaway jaw and eye sockets.

Pickings were good round the nearby close. The number of pumpkins and Happy Halloween banners showed Mrs Collins that she was in a minority here with her negative views of trick or treating. They targeted the pumpkin friendly dwellings, ignoring those in darkness. The streets were eerily quiet and they met only a few other brave sweet lovers willing to face the cold.

At 6 o'clock it was already pitch and apart from the faint glow of dwindling tea lights in subsiding pumpkins and intermittent street lights, it was a dark world. In this dark world Mrs Collins looked at her little troupe of ghouls and felt a prickle of fear down her back. Some of the costumes and make up were far too realistic. Then she saw Casey-Marie and remembered what she was doing.

Leaving number thirty-four with fresh sweet delights, Mrs Collins spotted a figure on the other side of the road. Death. The Grim Reaper. For a moment her heart stopped as she saw him raise his scythe. She gasped.

Then she realised - Kyle Ellis. She'd told him never to wear that outfit again, not after what had happened to Mr Robertson - surely he must be getting too tall for it soon anyway? And trust him to turn up late.

"Kyle Ellis, come over here and join the rest of us. Safely please- we always look when we cross – remember we have talked about road safety."

The Grim Reaper looked around as if not quite sure and then seemed to saunter across the road, not looking at all.

"Kyle Lewis, do your parents know that you are here? I'll be ringing them later - it's just not good enough to turn up late and in *that* costume. You'd better stay at the back with the … the alien superhero thing."

Death grunted. He certainly did look realistic. His masked face a cross between The Scream and a skeleton. Somehow the wrists and hands that protruded from wide sleeves looked skeletal too and bony fingers clenched an old- fashioned fob watch loudly ticking in one hand and the scythe in the other. A smear of blood edged the blade.

He looks even better than last year, Mrs Collins reluctantly admitted to herself.

Death took his place by chubby Casey- Marie at the back. Casey-Marie in her cheap, flammable costume, not realistic at all. Mrs Collins noticed that Death didn't seem that bothered about the sweets tonight, which was unusual for Kyle Ellis who already at his tender age had a dental hygiene issue due to poor diet. The other children were stuffing their mouths happily with chomp bars, chews and any other sweet delights they could get their hands on.

Oh well, thought Mrs Collins, *at least by the time they vomit they should be safely back in their own homes.*

As wispy dark grey clouds hung over a heavy sky, Mrs Collins led her troupe of merry halloweeners back to the church hall. They'd passed the hyper, from too much sugar, stage and were in a state of energy lacking slump, tired and grumpy on the side. They filed in to the cold church hall (how could it possibly feel colder inside than it did outside?) and compared and argued about amount of booty.

Mrs Collins tried to ignore the bickering, knowing that soon she could pass her young charges back to parents, who would be grateful that they hadn't had to endure the nightmare that is trick or treating.

"Sit down on the chairs for a minute, your parents will be arriving to pick you up soon. Hopefully."

The children obeyed collapsing wearily into the blue plastic chairs. They still somehow managed to have enough energy to keep stuffing handfuls of sweets into their mouths.

They look like overgrown cuckoos with those gaping mouths, thought Mrs Collins. *I'll be so glad when I've finished this job. It's not really for me. Oh well, Kyle Ellis- time to ring your parents.*

Mrs Collins got her mobile from her bag and found the emergency contact for the group of children.

"Hi yes, is that Kyle's dad? Oh sorry it's his mum is it? Well, I'd like to point out that it is not very helpful when Kyle turns up late. And in the costume that he was banned from wearing last year.

Please could you ensure…

Pardon? What? Kyle isn't well? He's in his bed with a sickness and …yes I understand…both ends. But that can't be… he's here.

Yes, I *would* like you to check that he's still in his room please. Yes, I will most certainly hold.

What? He is definitely in his room? Well…. No I don't need to hear the sound of him vomiting, I believe you. But then who is This Grim Reaper we have here then? No I do not expect you to answer that. It was a rhetorical question…

there's no need to be rude…

and good bye to you too."

Mrs Collins put down her phone and tried to spot Death. She caught sight of his dark grey cape behind Casey-Marie. Casey-Marie who was swinging her pumpkin in quite a fierce sort of way.

"Casey- Marie, please stop swinging that pumpkin, it's about to collapse into mush."

Casey-Marie was tired. She was especially grumpy. She hated her hodgepodge of a costume that was not as exciting as the other children's and she knew this was down to her mother who couldn't be bothered because she had her face buried in a gin bottle. Casey- Marie was especially jealous of the latecomer, that harbinger of doom, with his authentic spooky costume.

Casey-Marie did *not* stop swinging her pumpkin instead she swung it even higher and in the direction of Death himself. She swung it backwards and forwards, backwards and forwards, so high that it nearly bopped Death in the nose. Death gazed at her through the eye holes in his mask. The watch on his wrist seemed to beat loudly in time with her heart. Tick, tock, tick, tock. With a quick flick of his scythe, like swatting a fly, Death reflected the blow and sent pumpkin and candle straight back at Casey-Marie.

A spark from the nearly extinguished tea light flickered into life and ignited the cheap material of the half alien, half superhero costume. The child seemed rooted to the blue plastic chair. Her straggly black wig sparked into flame. Her flesh melted away like the plastic she was sitting on. Her body was ablaze. The other children and Mrs Collins watched in horror as within seconds Casey- Marie was engulfed in flames.

It was like they had frozen into stone. Until…Mrs Collins ran to the tap and dampened a tea towel (all she could find) flinging it over the child. Hardly daring to look at the charred thing that had until a minute ago been small, plump, unloved Casey-Marie.

Mrs Collins scrambled for the phone in her jacket and threw it at the tallest skeleton.

"Quick!" she shouted. "All of you, outside and phone 999. We've practised this, you know what to do."

In a zombie -like state the children staggered out of the hall, clustering in a group outside where the wailing began. Mrs Collins turned back to the child, or what was left of the child, the acrid smell of charred flesh filled her nostrils.

One figure remained. The Grim Reaper. He stood looking at the child's body with seemingly intense fascination. His heavy grey hood hung over his face.

"Who are you?"

He threw his head back and cackled in unearthly mirth. The hood fell back and the mask slid down, revealing a face with no skin, just a skull where maggots crawled and flies buzzed. Little bits of flesh clung to the bones. The rotting smell got stronger, entwined with the smell of sizzling flesh.

With intense horror Mrs Collins saw his skeleton body and a beating heart that pulsated in an empty rib cage. Brown intestines coiled in his belly like oozy, rancid snakes. Her legs gave way and she fell to the floor staring up at him. He leant over her and she curled into herself sure that her time was here.

"Ha, ha," he growled. "I must leave now, it's a busy night for me. This is the one night I can roam freely. See you soon."

At the doorway he paused.

"You should be ashamed of yourself, mistaking Kyle Ellis for me."

He left with a flourish of his cape, adjusting his hood and mask.

Mrs Collins curled up as tightly as possible and rocked and rocked and hummed and hummed. In the distance she heard the sound of a siren. Then the sickening thump of a speeding vehicle crashing and crumpling into a wall.

Further down the street The Grim Reaper extinguished the light from the eyes of the police driver and smiled to himself.

Adjudicator's feedback: It's not easy to combine comedy with horror, and few attempt it, but this author pulled it off and on the way produced one of the most different pieces amongst all the submissions. The dialogue was cleverly written and often hilarious (I wouldn't be surprised if the author was or has been a teacher in real life) resulting a very memorable piece. Unlike some of the other spooky surprises, this one was introduced more gradually, leaving you knowing more than the protagonist and willing her to catch on before something awful happened. Which of course it did!

Ten Thousand Hours of Love

by Robert Kibble

At what point, exactly, did you expect me to walk away?

You've got to remember what those times were like. We were just recovering from 7/7, and this was bloody Finsbury, and you know the shit that was going down. The bloody Daily Mail was going ape-crazy about radical this and radical that, and I was sent in to befriend her. Check out the charity. Find out whether it really was above board.

I swear I didn't plan what happened.

Her eyes got me, right off. It was like she was able to see right through me. Could have sworn she had me sussed right off, but she didn't say anything. Blue eyes, that light blue with a hint of darkness around, like that girl off the Time cover from Afghanistan years back. She looked at me, and a voice shouted in my head what are you doing here? Get out. I didn't listen, and you know what? I'm glad I didn't.

If I'd left then there'd have been no harm done, but I'd have walked away from the job, I'd have been finished, not that I'm not finished now. More importantly, someone else would have moved in to investigate her. We didn't trust those charities. They were good covers. And often they'd been used. Granted sometimes by our side, if we've got a side. God, I got pissed off when I heard about that polio charity being used to find Bin Laden. I mean, how stupid do you have to be? No wonder they don't trust us. We're so close to wiping it out, you know. Polio.

OK, OK. Digression.

It's painful.

I offered to help, volunteering, helping out with cleaning.

She ran this food bank / soup kitchen place off the high street, bringing people in and getting them sorted before sending them on their way, benefit forms in hand. The papers hated it. Boot camp for scroungers, one of them called it. I thought that too, but I didn't say, obviously. Playing the part. I'd even grown a beard to get in.

I started cleaning the dishes, so I was there, staying behind as she did the clearing up after everyone else had gone. We got chatting. Not comfortable, at first, because I was aware of those eyes, checking out my cover story. I'm good at inventing the little details, but even so – it's hard. Bloody hard keeping my background being the son of an asylum seeker who's sick of racism rather than a middle-class boy from Leicester who's sold out to the bloody cops.

You know two of my friends never spoke to me again once I said I was joining? Said I was like a Jew working for the Nazis. Said next time they saw me they'd "sort me out". Don't know what their problem was – it's not like we'd been harassed by police or anything. I know it happens, but that's why people like me should join up. To understand, you know? Different perspective.

Yeah, sorry.

We spent hours chatting, and it got comfortable. We got into playing this game, where we'd choose one of the people who'd been in and we'd make up a story about them. One day it was this old, white guy – we weren't discriminating or anything, she was good that way – and we made up this story about how he'd been a rich banker, and he'd lost it all so he'd walked out on his family in despair, so we'd have to be extra kind to him to build him up, so some day he'd see that he was worth it, and how they'd be happy to see him. It was nice making up the stories. The fact they weren't true made it easier – I wasn't lying any more.

I kept it together, knew what my job was, so I kept waiting

behind, kept her talking, and before you know it we were off to coffee shops, laughing, and she opened up. I thought now's the time. Now's when you find out if there's actually something going on or if this is all pukka. Now's when you get to the truth, make your report, and get out.

But I didn't want to.

I reported faithfully at first, reporting comings and goings, anyone "of interest" to us. There were a few, but if you saw how many people are technically on a watch-list – you don't know until you've been inside the system how many people we're watching in some way or another. That's what gets me when the press pick up on "why didn't they stop him – he was on a watch-list" – blimey, mate, half my cousins are on watch-lists, even the ones who haven't done anything.

Yeah, OK, back to her.

I knew in a couple of weeks that she was above board, but my reports had enough details of people who might be meeting there that it was worth me staying on, and as time went on... Well, maybe my reports left enough doubts about the men who'd been in that day, about which mosque they went to, about how she spent time talking with them alone. It was just enough, you know, just enough to give me an excuse to stay.

It was wrong. I know that. I deserve what's coming, don't think I don't know that, but I'm trying to explain how it was. If I went away, shaved my beard off, and came back saying who I really was... do you think she'd have welcomed me with open arms?

No.

We'd chatted about the police, you know, where she said she was sick of them picking on the downtrodden while they let the bankers get away with messing up the country. She was articulate about all that stuff – she'd done her reading. She knew what was what. Listened to people, read books. She had this thing she'd heard about Batman, how he picked on small time criminals on the street while ignoring big-time crooks and the real issues, and how he was a rubbish hero. We laughed about that. I think she'd got it from some comedian on TV, but she told it well. Better than I do. She was so funny. So alive. Those eyes, when she started going off on one, the way they darted back and forth, like she was connected to everything, like she could be the one to make a difference.

And she tried. Everyone was free to walk through those doors. She'd talk to each and every one of them – I didn't make that bit up. She'd listen, and she'd remember. She cared about every one of them. Even if she thought they could probably afford to go somewhere else. We'd had two of those guys – the ones the papers were probably right about – she said there was still something they needed, and besides, "better to feed a hundred undeserving than let one person starve". When she said it I believed it.

Yes, I loved her.

I really did.

I know it sounds a lie, given how things played out, but I did. I loved her so much, I couldn't help myself. I know how that sounds. I know I'm not the victim here. I'm trying to explain how it was.

She was the one who started it. Leaned over, stopped a fraction before her lips touched mine, looked up into my eyes, as if asking for permission – oh my god I was lost. We kissed, and then she leant back on her chair, looking satisfied. After a while: "I thought so."

I was terrified. Like that song, it's in his kiss – that one by Cher. I thought now she knows. I stared at her, and I must have shown it.

"What's the matter?" she asked. "Can't have been that much of a shock, can it?"

I laughed, a stupid laugh that was so fake, but she said nothing. My mouth felt dry. I took a sip of my coffee, half-choked trying to swallow it, coughed for about a minute, and then composed myself enough to speak, but I couldn't think of anything. Eventually I turned to her, leant over, and kissed her back, trying to make the situation seem normal.

It wasn't normal. Yes, I know. I could have pulled away, but I didn't. I couldn't. No. I didn't want to.

We went back to hers that night, and I didn't leave all weekend.

Every time she left the room… was she going to find someone to come and beat the shit out of me, walk out, phone the police… I don't know. Every time. That voice in my head was screaming, but that weekend I screamed back at it, falling into bed with her, kissing her, loving her.

Yes, I know I was playing a role, but it was me underneath. The me that kissed her – that was real. That was real love. That was something special. That's not something I've ever felt before. I relished every second of her time with me. I lapped up every word she said. I hear them, even now. That's why I kept her photo. Which is why you bastards know.

Whatever you do to me, know that I loved her. That whole year we spent together, me writing desperate reports back to stay on the case, them slowly catching up with me, my eventual transfer coming closer and closer. I worked it out. We spent one year, one month, and three weeks between that first kiss and me having to leave, when I got pulled. Just over ten thousand hours we spent together, and that's more than some people get, so no, I don't regret it.

I regret not having the balls to tell her, but when could I?

If I'd told her at the beginning we'd not have had what we had.

If I'd told her part-way through, she wouldn't have said "Oh well, that's fine, I love you for who you are" when she didn't know me from Adam. Well, she did. She knew me. I was true to her, how I felt about her.

Yes, I know I didn't tell her my real name. Lots of people change their names. Lots of people walk out on their partners. Lots of men leave. I didn't cheat on her, I haven't even had a relationship since. I didn't lie to her about anything that mattered to me.

Yes, I know it sounds pathetic. Do you know how many times I went back to that soup kitchen and watched, watching her lock up? I thought about rushing up, confessing everything. I wanted her to turn round and recognise me. I wanted her to run up, shout at me, curse me, attack me, anything.

But I put it off, one day to the next, until one day she didn't appear.

The street was empty that morning, and the next, and yeah, now you tell me that's because she moved back home to have the baby, and if I'd known…

I don't know.

And now here I am. Back where it all began, where you guys – or people like you – gave me the order to go off and distrust people, to pretend to be something I wasn't. Well, maybe a policeman was what I wasn't. Maybe that was the lie all along. I'm not one now, but I still remember her. I had ten thousand hours with the finest woman ever to walk the planet, and if you're asking me am I sorry about that, then no. I'm not.

If you say I broke the law, I broke the law. If you're saying I deserved to be fired, then fine, you've got me. If you say I'm a pathetic loser who should have owned up and taken my chance with the best woman I'll ever meet, that's true too.

But don't ever ask me to say I didn't truly love her, because that, more than anything else, would be the real crime.

Adjudicator's feedback: A most engaging contemporary story and the only one in my top ten to feature a spy as a spook

70

– and a most unusual one at that. Instantly believable, it was hard to know how the tale would resolve which made it a gripping read to the end. An excruciating dilemma faced by the narrator was bound to arrive and yet was skilfully handled and heart-wrenching. One of the most memorable and unusual stories of the competition.

These Damn Conspirators of Hell

by Phillip Vine

Once, I did a heinous thing.

I don't expect you to love me or even to feel sorry for me but it will help me in my tormented state if I can be certain you will read my story.

You will know of my success, my fame, and my wealth, but you will not know of my unhappiness – which celebrity and its close attendants affluence and avarice so often bring with them – and of my terror – which crime and its close attendants guilt and ghosts so often bring with them too.

Above all, I need you to understand, I beg of you to try.

I was not always thus.

My origins were humble but insufficiently so for you to pity me.

I was born in Cambridge, but on the wrong side of the tracks, as they say, in Romsey Town, which has a certain reputation. My father was employed by the London and North Eastern Railway, maintenance work mostly, earning overtime on Sundays and Bank Holidays when the trains to Liverpool Street ran less frequently or not at all. My mother was a shop worker, selling silk sheets in Eaden Lilley's to the privileged, and it made her sick to do so. Sometimes she beat me, I am convinced, because of her sickness, her jealousy of the feckless rich.

But most or almost all of this is in the public domain.

My marital woes I have been less keen to publicise, for the obvious reason they show me in a far from advantageous light. My first wife, in fact, I beat with my fists in my frustration, and there you have a fact so far hidden from public view.

I am now alone and, probably, deservedly so.

Apart, that is, from my thoughts that sting like wasps and occasional sightings of persons from the past.

It seems incredible now that once I was a failing writer.

True enough, Faber had published a slim volume of my poetry, and various quarterlies had featured a handful of short stories. There had even been one novel, since pulped at my express command, though, unfortunately, second hand copies are still available on Amazon at extortionate prices.

In stark contrast, the talent of my best friend, Jack Tomson, was sublime.

He enjoyed all the gifts – sensitivity to tortured souls, a poetic turn of phrase, a compelling sense of story, a rhythm to his writing that carried readers to whatever place and time he wished to explore.

His books sold in their millions, but he did endure some ugly disadvantages.

One was his cancer and two was his friendship with me.

And three was his lack of belief in his own abilities.

The disease feasted on his lungs and killed him painfully whereas I betrayed his trust.

And it was his diffidence, his reticence that played into my undeserving hands.

When Jack was informed by a callous doctor that he had less than one year to live, he asked me to be his literary executor, and confessed that he had three almost completed novels that he'd been afraid to show his editor at Random House. They were *serious* works, *literary* works, and he was unsure of their reception either by his publisher or by the public.

'You'll do it for me, Micky, won't you?'

His voice already seemed ethereal, ghostly.

I nodded my assent.

At that time, I would have done anything for my friend, who dutifully read my dull manuscripts and tried to breathe some kind of life into them, but I have to confess my interest was especially piqued, twisted, by news of the unpublished writings.

What exactly would I do with them when Jack was gone?

'I'll leave it all to you, Micky.'

Jack Tomson was a trusting soul.

After a decent interval, I told him he'd been wise to keep his unpublished work under wraps.

Of course, you now understand only too well what I did once my friend was gone.

My theft – although I told myself it was a borrowing – of Jack's novels brought me fame and fortune beyond my wildest calculations.

I revealed one of my deceased friend's novels every two years – each requiring only the addition of a few words here and a few words there, tasks even my limited skills could not spoil – and then I told my publisher I could write no more.

'Well, it's a shame,' he said. 'But your reputation is secure, your novels are already part of the canon.'

I recall I nodded in smug acceptance of the accolade from the man with the huge glass fronted office at Random House.

I retired to the Cambridgeshire countryside, to a house in Barrington with a reputation for ghosts.

I was old enough now, I told myself, not to believe in hauntings.

During the following years, I earned an increasing reputation as a recluse. I granted the occasional interview to aspiring journalists, ones who would not ask tough questions, ones who would not dare to question how I had made the transition from the dire, mostly pulped *Outward Bound* – now trading on Amazon at £456 for a first and only edition – to the magisterial trilogy, *Hot and Cold Lives.*

I lived alone – save for a woman from the village who came in twice a week to cook and clean – and save from the visit of an occasional woman of the night from Cambridge – and saw not one ghost for many years.

It was a prosaic existence, but one that suited me well, late breakfast and pots of black coffee, perusal of *The Times*, wine and fresh salmon for lunch. I enjoyed walks about the banks of the meandering River Cam, and reading in the summer house at the foot of my garden until the fading of the light forced me inside to enjoy the delights prepared for me by Mrs Potts.

Once I re-read one of Jack's science fiction adventures – *Deep Space, Deep Time*, if my memory serves – but it was not a patch on any of the novels I had crafted from his manuscripts.

I wished Jack Tomson well wherever and whenever his next life took him.

When I thought about my borrowings, I felt no guilt at all. My former friend had lacked the genius to recognise his genius. I had served the commonwealth of writers and readers to the best of my ability in bringing his work to the attention of the world at large.

All was well for years until the visit of my younger sister to Barrington House.

She was the last person I would have expected as she had been dead for ten years at least.

'Laura,' I said – trying to retain at least a semblance of composure – 'what a – nice – surprise to see you.'

She was lying on my bed, the quilt turned back, naked as the day she was born, bloodied as the day she died.

I had gone upstairs to fetch a book – Shirley Jackson's *The*

Haunting of Hill House, as it happens, which made me think I was imagining my unexpected visitor.

I retained no such illusion once I saw the blood from her neck seeping on to my newly laundered pillow. It was exactly as I remembered – Laura's neck not my pillow – with bright red roses of blood blooming from the jagged saw of her wound.

(You see how limited, how hackneyed is my imagery when I have nothing but my own devices upon which to rely.)

I studied the wraith of my sister until she broke the silence between us.

'You,' she said, and the word was deep and accusatory.

I nodded in acceptance of my guilt.

'I had no choice,' I said, 'once I knew you knew.'

'I wouldn't have breathed a word,' she said.

But how could I have trusted her? How was I to be sure she would not have called a press conference to denounce my plagiarism before the unforgiving world?

'You knew you could have relied on me, Micky.'

I ran from the bedroom, pell-mell, head-first, break-neck down the stairs.

I suspect Jack Tomson was involved somehow in my death, but his complicity was difficult to prove.

It was the means of my end that made me suspicious.

If you have read the closing lines of the final volume of Jack's – or rather my – trilogy, you will appreciate my former friend's views on life after death, and of his incorporation of the retributory work of ghosts into his – my – literary fiction.

I won't say more, as I have sufficient sins about my soul without adding a further by revealing the climax of a wonder-ful work of art which you may not yet have read.

I will admit, though, that it was a heinous thing I had done, this murder of my sister.

It is – I have been told – the reason for my captivity here.

On my arrival, I asked – nay begged – for three concessions in my incarceration. One, a pen and paper on which to script this confession.

Two, copies of *The Times* to be delivered to my cell until such a time as my obituary had been published.

(You see how my ego is undiminished, even unto death.)

Three, the freedom – at nightfall – to roam the highways of hell in search of my sister, Laura, and my former friend, Jack Tomson.

(You see how the desire for vengeance remains to torture us, to curse us, those of us at least who have sinned greatly.)

I wondered now whether Jack had been my friend at all.

I suspected he had been in league with Laura all along, that my sister's spectral corpse had paid court to Jack's decomposing flesh, that she had responded to his advances, that she had dragged him down to hell. I imagined she had whispered sweet nothing lies about my theft of Jack's manuscripts in his rotting ears.

I had no choice, once dark had dimmed the fires here, but to seek them out, these damned conspirators of hell.

The way was narrow, a passageway underground, with everywhere the sweet smell of decomposition, of damp earth and of insatiable worms.

Sometimes I was forced to crawl on hands and knees but my thirst for retribution was too strong, my need for *haunting* so overwhelming, I could do nothing but continue through this limbo between the twin worlds of hell and heaven.

I had no idea until now that ghosts had no choice but to hunt – a word so closely related to *haunt*.

I had no choice but to find Laura and Jack and do what I had to do.

That they would be together, I had no doubt.

When the darkness in the tunnel began to lighten, I understood that I was approaching the gates of heaven.

I knew *they* would be there.

Waiting.

Bathed in ethereal light of a quality impossible to describe, I saw my sister and my former friend, held in each other's arms, each other's smiles, both restored in body and in soul.

I moved towards them, to haunt, to hunt.

And was prevented from doing so by some invisible force field that I later understood to be the love of God.

(You see how I may have mellowed in the years.)

(You see how I crave your compassion.)

(You see how I am condemned to fail.)

Adjudicator's feedback: I love a story like this where the first person narrator talks directly to you, the reader, from the start and is clearly in anguish. Clever use of asides in parentheses now and again keeps this direct relationship between reader and writer closely alive as the striking tale unfurls and the tension builds. The spookiness is not a sudden revelation, like many of the other submissions, but the horror manages to continue to build throughout – not an easy task. Written with originality and style.

Longlisted

Ruth Flanagan
Joseph Francis McCullough
Phillip Vine
Maureen Nisbet
Stephanie Makins
Colin Sheehan
Jonathan Sean Lyster
Phyllida Scrivens
Jacqueline Fowle
Jeni Lawes

MEMBERS CHALLENGE SHIELD

Foreword

Holly Ainley

It has been such an interesting process and indeed a pleasure to read and judge the entries for this year's Olga Sinclair Member's Shield challenge.

Reading the 15 entries, I experienced a whole gamut of emotions and reading experiences, finding passion, drama, surprise, provocation, plenty of darkness, as well as points of real humour, enjoyment and tenderness.

I want to take a moment to recognise not only the skill but the courage it takes to share a new piece of writing and to lay it open to critique and feedback. Since you are all part of the Writer's Circle and will all have cultivated strong working, writing relationships, you will know what an effect this process of sharing can have, both on an individual piece but also on your overall development and confidence as a writer. I say this by way of thanking you, for letting me be part of the process in this instance.

My experience of working in different parts of the book trade – from editorial to where I am now as a book buyer and bookseller – means I understand both the joys and the great challenges authors face in moving from a place of very personal creativity, to something public and open to scrutiny. And without doubt, the authors I know with the strongest sense of purpose, level-headedness and enjoyment in their work, are those who continually challenge themselves by work shopping, discussing, entering their works-in-progress to competitions like this, and using every opportunity to hone their skill. So, congratulations to everyone who entered – I am full of awe and appreciation for what you do and what you have shared.

For me one of the greatest pleasures of being involved in this challenge was the opportunity to immerse myself in stories that were, for want of a better word, 'raw' – not that they were unfinished or roughly composed but that they still had the newness and freshness of an original thought. And though not every story could be a winner, I certainly found real variety in the styles, voices, settings and characters you all created.

To echo what I said back in April, some of the central facets in each story that I paid particular attention to were: the setting – and how a sense of place can influence a character's behaviour. Hand in hand with this was the atmosphere – that intangible combination of mood and setting that that gives a story a particular tone – something hard to do within the limited word count of a short story. And then the immediacy of voice – again, with this medium, it's essential to engage the reader from line one. This didn't mean I was looking for fireworks in the opening sentence but rather I wanted to feel a sense of authorial control and direction from the word go – to instantly connect with the narrative voice.

Of course, I also took into account the way in which this year's theme had been interpreted and incorporated. Beyond crafting of the stories, I think writing to a theme was a big part of this challenge – to use it as a springboard rather than to be bound by it; to make it part of the fabric of the story rather than have it signalled or signposted too obviously. Some of the stories were more successful in this regard than others but every one of them responded to the notion of 'Spooks' with aplomb.

I read of ghosts – those that haunted on a bleak and rainy moor, to a more positive force that came to the rescue in a moment of need for a young family on a boating holiday on the Broads. There were spooks from old legend: selkies, Black Shuck and the terrifying, murderous spirit of Frau Perchta in Austria. Characters sprang up, from an old Norwich weaver, to a murderous crime writer, four teenagers tragically killed at sea, intolerant pub landlords, a young woman groomed as a Russian spy and a junior at a solicitor's firm who faced a long, dark night of the soul after stealing a ream of copy paper. Stories were contemporary and historical. Boris Johnson made a noteworthy appearance, as did death himself, on Halloween.

I hope this gives you a flavour of the great range of ideas and styles entered this year. It meant that the judging wasn't easy and as with most good fiction, the winning stories also contain a more unpredictable, hard to pin down ingredient. It is that spark you feel as a reader when you find yourself immersed in a story; for a moment, not even thinking about the technicalities of it but purely being swept along. Because after all, isn't this why we read fiction? To look outside of our view of the world and be temporarily transported elsewhere, learning, being challenged, and sometimes coming back to ourselves enriched, maybe even a little changed.

In the winning entries this year I experienced this moment of immersion and in the winner, I felt it carried through the whole story. Though each of the 15 entries can be commended for showing skill in many of the areas I've mentioned, for me the third, second and first prize came closest to balancing them all in such a way I could relax and stop looking for them anymore. None of the stories is perfect, but I don't think that was the object of this competition and anyway, fiction is subjective – rather that the top three entries I would love to read more of, were they to be extended, edited or used as inspiration for a broader collection.

1ˢᵗ Place

The Serenity of Still Water

by Iain Andrews

Adjudicator's feedback: This is a sharp, confident story with an impressively executed twist in the very last few lines. It's not easy to create a successfully unreliable narrator but here is a perfect example: from the start the narrative voice hooks the reader into the story, eliciting sympathy, then fear, before turning things on their head with a big reveal. Overall the writing is atmospheric, with a strong sense of unease throughout and the story manages to entwine myth, ghosts, crime and thriller elements whilst never feeling over-stretched or rushed. Congratulations!

2nd place

How to Become a Spook

by Anne Funnell

Dorcas Lawson was sweeping out the bin floor of the Weybourne Post Mill. She had to flick the grains and husks into a pile while letting the rubbish blow away in the gentle breeze from the open shutter. She was startled by someone banging on the ladder. She looked out and saw the Boy John on the ground.

"I'm up here," she shouted.

"Gotta... message for... your Dad." John had been running and was out of breath.

"He's not here. Tell me."

"It's orders. 'Bout his cart."

This meant it was a serious, private message. "I'll come down." The inside ladder from the floor where the wheat was stored was, like the mill itself, over a hundred years old and rickety. John had the sense to jump onto the outside ladder, a foot above the ground, and come up the steps towards the double doors, which Dorcas kept closed.

Face to face, John held up his left hand, spreading his fingers. "Carts wanted for the run tonight. I got five promised. Your Dad will ha' to take his down to the beach."

"Six? Are you sure? Thass a big run."

86

John held up his right forefinger. "Thass what he said. Five and one is six."

"What time?"

"Moonrise is midnight. Gotta be away by then."

"He's gone up to Brewer Britolph with the flour. You'll have to go up to there and tell them the cart's wanted down here for the run."

Dorcas knew there'd be a fuss if the cart hadn't been unloaded and the flour put away. But Mr Britolph profited from the brandy landed on the beach, and his boss was the land agent, Jennis Johnson, who must have arranged with the smugglers for the run on 28th February, a long black night. Weybourne Hope had been a landing place since Roman times because shallow draught vessels could stretch mooring lines up the beach and unload sacks or barrels onto a cart standing on the shingle.

Dorcas abandoned the sack of feed for her hens, shut the double doors, and began to run down Beach Lane to the watermill. Both the mills belonged to Mr Britolph and had been made, if legends were believed, by the monks of the priory long since robbed of every useful bit of stone leaving just the rubble of flint in a maze of walls.

The mill was quiet although a little trickle fell over the boards holding back the water in the pond. This mill could only run for a short while before the water became too low. The postmill could only run if the wind was south of west. So grinding was on-and-off work for her father. Dorcas made sure the inside was ready to receive anything which wouldn't fit onto the carts, and have to be hidden in the mill until the barrels or sacks of tea, coffee or tobacco could be taken safely away.

She then went down the lane, past the end of the cliff and onto the shingle. She called, "Stefan?"

He appeared from his shelter, an untidy collection of drift-wood and canvas, mostly hidden under falls from the chalk cliffs. He was a castaway himself, for his father's Dutch fishing boat had been wrecked on the offshore reef. His father drowned because he was wearing oilskins and boots. Stefan survived because, unusually for a sailor, he could swim and boys never wore sea-boots. He now made a living by helping the Weybourne fishermen haul their boats up beyond high tide mark and he mended their nets or sails.

Dorcas told him of the run, but Stefan knew all about it, and said, "I bin told the Revenue cutter is in Wells harbour. Having its sails tarred."

"Why?"

"So's it dunt show up in the gloom."

"Will they be safe?" She meant the smugglers. "Moonrise is after midnight."

"Nother bitta gossip. Revenue gotta troop of horses to ride along the cliffs."

"I can't do anything about them."

"Yes, you can. Pretend to be a spook."

"A what?"

"Dutch word. Means a spy. You know, how a horse is spooked by a dog inna hedge. Hide up. Jump out. Like I do." Stefan had a cloak made of tattered strips of canvas and a bonnet much the same to frighten unwanted snoopers.

Dorcas walked up the lane, thinking of how she could spook a horse in the dark. Her skirt was rustic home weave, and her jacket was un-bleached linen. She stopped by the post-mill. The four sails had been set at rest, on the diagonal. Too late to set them as a warning - on the cross. No. She needed her long white skirt and shawl to flap at a rider coming down the Furl, the track from the cliff-top to the bridge over the leat. That meant going up to their cottage. Her father, Albert Lawson, did odd jobs for Lady Cook's Land Agent, Jennis Johnson, and as a carter was granted a tied cottage. Dorcas hoped that Lady Cook, a widow who'd inherited the estate, would be safely inside her own house, and that she could slip in, get the clothes, a bottle of ale, and some bread, cheese and an apple, and sneak out without being seen and interrogated.

It was a forlorn hope. Lady Cook must have been alerted by the request for carts, and was on the watch.

"Where are you going, my girl, at this time of night?"

"I came to get some food for my Dad. There's to be a run."

"Of course, I blame your mother," the lady said in her supercilious tones.

"What for? Dad helping the smugglers?" Not, surely for dying after my brother was born, she thought. An unwanted heir who'd died the same day.

"No! For marrying beneath her."

"She loved my father and he was broken up after her death." She thought it unlikely that her mother would have been diverted from the path of true love, for Dorcas had been accused of inheriting that stubborn streak.

"So he may have been, but she educated you above your station."

"Yes, Grandmother." Dorcas dropped a curtsey, intending to provoke and divert suspicion.

"Do not call me that!"

"No, my Lady."

Lady Cook swirled away in a flurry of silk and ribbons. That's the way to do it, Dorcas thought. Swirl.

Five requisitioned carts passed quietly down Beach Lane, surfaced with white sand over the pebbles, the hoofs muffled and the axles well-greased. No lights were needed, sufficient came from the night sky, reflected on the flint walls. It seemed hours before Alfred Lawson came by, and waved to his daughter standing on the ladder up to the mill.

"Are you orlright, lass?"

'Go on down with the cart, Dad. I bin put on watch here, case of riders."

"Too dark for them, surely?"

"Talk to Stefan. Then come back. I got food."

"There'll be plenty down there, the lads had warning."

Dorcas knew that there would be bits of news to exchange while they covered up the carts, unharnessed the ponies, fed and watered them for a wait of several hours. Some of the incoming boats would have their own unloading tackle. Even so, those on the beach needed to be ready to rig an A-frame with a pulley to swing sacks of precious dry stuff like tea or tobacco over the waves.

The last flush of the setting sun over the Wash sank below the black horizon. Now she must get to the top of the postmill, open the little hatch and arrange herself to stay on watch for a rider on the hill-top. Oh, wait. Put the swirling skirt and shawl on. What about her face? A little bit of flour and water? No… Ale… mixed in the hand and wiped on her face.

Still not right. The view out of the hatch looked up the lane. Cautiously, she crept down the first rickety ladder, lifted up the hatch in the grinding floor, down the next ladder, out through the double doors and down the stairs. She would have to move the whole mill on its post by pushing the wheel several yards up hill. It usually took two people, one to hold the steps up with a lever, and the other to push on the beam which was supported on a cart wheel.

She was startled by a low coo-ee from behind her. She swung around, the skirt swirling out.

"Perfect spooking dress," Stefan said. "Just cum to see you orlright?"

"Perfect timing," she replied. "I just need the hatch at the top facing a bit more up the hill."

This they managed. Stefan lifted the steps, and Dorcas pushed the cart wheel round until the mill had turned several points anti-clockwise.

Now it was up to her to keep awake. Spook any riders from the east. There was a faint green glow in the otherwise dark sky. Her school mistress said it was The Northern Lights. The Aurora Borealis. Seamen had seen them flickering green and dancing violet when fishing off Norway. Nothing to be afraid of. Useful, in fact, tonight as a horse on the hill would be visible. If she kept her eyes open.

A clatter of iron-shod hoofs on the bridge shocked her alert. In a panic she jumped down the top ladder, holding up her skirts in one hand, through the hatch, round and down onto the next ladder, caught her foot in the long cloth as she opened the doors, tumbled onto the top of the steps and screeched in alarm as she felt herself falling. She hit the ground with a heavy thump, and lay there winded. Her shawl slowly floated down after her.

She was only vaguely aware of trampling hoofs near her head, a horse neighing in fright, and a bang as something crashed into the beam.

The flashes of lights behind her eyes gradually faded. She opened her eyes and her night-vision returned sufficiently for her to see a head on the grass. She managed to get an arm under her shoulder. No. Not a head. A helmet of some sort, glints of brass on a chin-strap. Riding Officers were paid from the value of the goods they seized. They were hated as informers, intent on disrupting what the smugglers regarded as their necessary trade.

Even so, a human being, hurt and lying on the ground, groaning in pain. She was cautious, for he might be armed with a pistol or musket.

She felt her way towards the body, murmuring, "All right there?"

He, like herself, had been knocked out, but recovered enough to sit up, holding his head. "You spooked my horse."

She wished she could say, "Yes. That's what I was supposed to do." Instead she put his helmet into his lap. "I'll go fetch him."

The apple core in her pocket proved to be the right bribe to overcome his fright. Dorcas held the reins while the officer remounted, grumbling.

She must try another ploy. "I'll set you on your way." She walked towards the Priory ruins, stepping out of her encumbering skirt, dropping it behind her in a bush. She wiped the dried flour mask off her face, letting the reins slip through her fingers. She said, "Walk on," to the horse, bent low, and slid sideways into a gap.

The horse, obediently, continued for he could see, better than a man in the dark, the way out onto the coast road to Sheringham and his barracks.

Dorcas did not move out of hiding until she heard his hoofs on the hard surface of the highway. The officer, probably still dazed, made no fuss. She wondered if he would tell his Captain he had been spooked off his horse or if he would be dishonest and lie: "Duty done. Nothing to see."

Either way, she had saved the run.

Adjudicator's feedback: The only entry with an entirely historical setting, I loved the understated interpretation of the theme here, with young Dorcas Lawson 'spooking' the watchman's horse in order to protect her father's smuggling efforts. For me this was had the most literary edge, with an absorbing, well-researched backdrop, full of historical detail yet retaining a lightness and sense of fun. I have a slight hesitation about the decision to portray Norfolk dialect on the page, but this is personal preference and overall it doesn't detract from the well-rounded characters and lovely depiction of working life in the period.

3rd place

Childhood Haunts

by Jon Platten

Gravel crunched beneath his feet. From somewhere in the monochrome landscape, bonfire fragrances tickled his throat. Smoke blended with the mist that skulked out of the nearby woods, devious and sinister, concealing the path through the cemetery. Ahead, he could see a silent figure emerge from the vapour. It couldn't be him. Could it?

The town was taller back then. The pavement closer, its cracks describing an imaginary network of rivers and roads. The route home from his primary school, in reality just a few hundred yards, was to Billy a trek along the edge of the unknown, through a labyrinth of dull orange brick Victorian villas.

'I came top in English today, Mum…'

'Oh did you? What a good boy.'

'But Robert says he won't invite me to his party now. And no-one wants to sit at my table.'

'Take no notice, my dear, they're only jealous.'

The quick pace was making Billy breathless.

'Hold my hand, dear, it will be alright.'

Billy reached for his mother's hand. Connected, nothing

could scare him now as he strode along the twilit streets. At home, a plate of spaghetti hoops on toast and the chance to watch *Crackerjack!* or read alone in his bedroom awaited him. By reading, he'd get ahead in his school tests, he would 'get on'. 'Education,' his mother said, would give him 'the best start in life'.

'Terry, we're back!'

'Oh. When's tea?'

'Soon. Billy's got something to tell you, dear.'

'He has, has he? I thought children should be seen and not heard.'

'Don't be like that, dear. He came top in English.'

'Oh.'

'I just need to pop upstairs, Terry. Put tea on, won't you?'

Billy's dad sighed as he got up from his chair to go to the kitchen cupboard. He handed Billy the tin-opener and can of spaghetti hoops. Billy fumbled with what seemed like a hand-held metallic puzzle. He tried a few manoeuvres but the tin resisted them all.

'You've not even made an impression.'

Billy's dad wrenched the kitchen implement off him. With a stab and a twist, he opened the tin and poured the contents into a saucepan.

Tea was eaten in silence. Then Billy got his chance to read.

Billy was relieved to make out his student room as he awoke from a dream about mountaineering. The sound of Duran Duran's latest single from his clock radio eased the fear he had felt at the sight of the rockface – easy to climb, but impossible to descend. His room was now completely characterless. Details that had marked it out as his were now either packed in a bulging suitcase or squashed into bin bags awaiting collection on the landing. He could not believe that this was his last day in a place that had become more like home than home.

University had come and gone. He stood on the threshold of a future that shimmered with endless possibilities.

Sarah was already up.

'When's your train again?' She asked.

'Not till this afternoon. We've plenty of time.'

'What about lunch at The Eagle? Celebrate that first-class degree.'

'Er…Don't think so, no. I can't stand any more goodbyes.'

'Louisa will be there.' Sarah was standing over Billy now, hands on hips.

Louisa. Three syllables. Infinite memories. Her teacher had even put something similar on her report: 'Age cannot wither her, nor custom stale her infinite variety'. Billy's tutors had made it clear that you couldn't write reports like that. Not in the state school where he was about to start his teaching career.

'What's she doing next, anyway?' asked Sarah.

'Well…apparently, her dad's got her a job in the City, whatever that means. Starting salary of twenty grand.'

'Twenty grand? Wow. She's fallen on her feet.' Billy struggled to assess the level of bitterness in Sarah's reaction.

'Oh Sarah, stop going on about her. She's history.'

'Ancient history or modern history?'

'Hah. You know the university defines modern history as starting with the decline of the Roman Empire, so technically…'

'I'm teasing, silly…'

'Yeah, I know. Let's go out for breakfast.

'Love you.'

'Love you too. Till we're old and grey.'

'Till we're old and grey.'

Billy glimpsed a blur in the corner of his eye just before the Oxford Mathematical Instruments tin crashed against the classroom wall, scattering its contents among the desks. Jenny, the stationery set's owner, flushed red but held back the tears. She could not show weakness. Instead, she looked to her new teacher to make an impression on the class.

'Er...Who threw that?'

Laughter.

'It was Jenny, sir, it's her stuff.'

Billy could not see who had said this. He had been trying to get the video to work. Whilst his back had been turned, the class had grown restless. He thought it was one of the lads at the back. He hadn't mastered their names yet, an ignorance compounded by the uniform appearance of twelve-year olds in the 1980s: mullet haircuts, white socks, cardigans.

'Who did that?' Billy's voice came out more reedy than he wanted.

'Who did that?' repeated a chorus from the back of the class, higher-pitched and more nasal, devastatingly accurate in its mimicry.

'Someone will end up in detention...' He tried again.

'Someone will end up in detention,' came the echo.

'Look...'

'Look.'

Silence.

'What are we supposed to be looking at?'

Laughter.

A bell broke the stand-off.

'Before anyone leaves the class...'

But the class were already leaving, some running, others sauntering. Jenny was the last to leave.

'Sir?'

'Yes, Jenny?'

'You're a rubbish teacher.'

Billy walked down the road to the phone box with a pocketful of 10p coins. He hauled the door open, to be greeted by the sour smell of stale urine and a temperature that contrived to be colder than it was outside. Carefully, he dialled the number. He hoped his mother answered.

'Oh it's you. I thought you'd left home. Couldn't keep away, could you? I'll put you on to your mother...'

'Hello my dear, how's it going?'

'Yeah, fine, thanks,' he lied.

I knew you'd be ok. Born to it, my dear, born to it.'

'Yeah.'

Billy searched for something to say but it was his mother who broke the stalemate:

'Anything else?'

'Er...not really. You ok?'

'Oh yes, my dear, I'm fine. Getting ready to go on holiday.'

'Er. That's nice. Where to?'

'Scarborough, same as usual.'

'Scarborough. That's nice. The pips are going. I'll have to go. Bye.'

'Goodbye my dear, goodbye...'

He couldn't tell her. Couldn't tell her that he was spending his days being humiliated by children half his age who refused to do anything he said. She wouldn't understand. In her classroom, her word was law. From that distance, she couldn't help.

Billy searched the college lawn for any familiar face. Thirty years on, this was quite ambitious. He knew it was a mistake to go back to his old university. Suddenly, right next to him, he saw someone he recognised from Facebook.

'Matt!'

'Hey... Graham isn't it?'

'Er...It's Billy, actually...'

'Billy, yah, I remember. So what did you end up doing?'

'I went into teaching.'

98

'Oh. Right. Is that what you wanted?'

'Yeah. I was lucky. I always knew what I wanted to do...'

'Really? How come?' Matt sipped his wine whilst scanning the other groups scattered about the college lawn.

'Er...I suppose my mum was a teacher, I liked the structure, I wanted to do something with my degree that would make a difference...'

'That's a real...privilege, I guess. Don't know if I could deal with all those spotty teenagers myself.'

'Er...Yeah...What about you?'

'Journalism.'

'Oh. How did that go?'

'Great. Went all over the world. Met some incredible people...'

'Really? Sounds great.'

The jazz band struck up.

'Like who?'

'Oh... John McEnroe... Lewis Hamilton. Sports personalities mostly.'

'Wow. That's incredible.'

The two men paused to concentrate on the complex task of simultaneously doing three things with two hands: balancing a wine glass, holding a plate and picking up a crust-less smoked salmon sandwich to eat. Billy desperately tried to think of something to say to keep the conversation going.

It was Matt who spoke first.

'So you got to be headteacher, right?'

'Er...No...I had an interview for deputy head...'

'Oh...'

The two men chewed.

'But I was happy teaching, really, spending time with the kids.'

'I see...'

Another pause. Again, broken by Matt.

'Did you keep seeing…Louisa, wasn't it?'

'Yeah. No, not Louisa. Sarah. We split up in my probationary year – the first year of teaching. We didn't really see much of each other, what with all my marking and lesson preparation. And her job was quite a long way from where I was living…'

But Matt was now catching up with the couple to his right.

The headteacher's office seemed smaller with the governors shoehorned around the table. Billy had found the interview testing but he felt confident in his responses. As the headteacher came to his final questions, tension seemed to leave the room like air from an old balloon.

'So Billy, tell us why you feel you would be the right person for the post of deputy headteacher?'

'Er… Well, my qualifications are excellent. I have a good rapport with the children. The younger teachers often approach me for advice and I'm happy to give it.'

'But you've only worked *here*, haven't you? There are candidates who've worked elsewhere, who could bring new ideas to the school. Cross-fertilisation.'

'I… I accept that… But I've kept my training record up to date. As you'll see from my application form, I got a Master's Degree in Education Leadership. My school-based project led to a 25% improvement in boys' English exam results.'

'Mmmm. Is there anything else you'd like to say?'

'Well, as you know, my health is generally good. I think I've only had one day off in the last seven years. I'm conscientious, reliable. I'm usually the first person here and the last to leave. I contribute to extra-curricular activity. The choir I run has had some lovely comments from parents and the football team have really improved.'

'OK. Anything else?'

'Er…No…I think that's it.'

'In which case, thank you very much, Billy.'

Billy said his thankyous and walked out of the room. Seen and not heard.

Gravel crunched beneath his feet. Old and grey, Billy stands at the grave, chrysanthemums dangling in his hand. Through the fog and smoke he sees… it can't be. His father? It's him, but with a full head of hair and the swagger of youth. How come? His body spasms with the recognition. A familiar snide voice brings him up short.

'I knew you couldn't keep away.'

'I…'

'Don't know why you've bothered, mind. I don't want you here. Haven't you got anything better to do?'

'Er…I thought…'

'That was always your problem. Thinking. Waste of time. Should have spent your time doing.'

'I've come to…'

'I know why you've come. She's not here.'

'I never expected…'

'I never expected…' his father repeats his words in a high-pitched nasal echo. 'Your head was always in the clouds. Or in a book. Same thing really. Made an impression yet?'

He knew it was a mistake. Billy is sixty years old. His father would have been… how old? But he seemed younger. How was that possible? Speaking to Billy just like he did when he was a child.

The memory is too painful. He can't fight the tears. To his father, he was always a failure. Through tear-blurred eyes, the cemetery takes on the appearance of an impressionist painting.

He stands at the grave, chrysanthemums dangling in his hand. Chrysanthemums, her favourite flowers.

'Take no notice, my dear, he's only jealous.'

Billy looks up.

'Mum!'

'Hello my dear. I knew you couldn't keep away.'

Billy's tears return.

'Hold my hand, my dear, it will be alright.'

Billy reaches out. But she turns, and is gone.

A breath.

Heard but not seen.

Adjudicator's feedback: I was struck by the assured use of time in the story, moving convincingly as it does from a man's childhood to old age in a few paragraphs. This is ambitious with so few words, yet it works, portraying Billy's life, developing a clear, convincing protagonist who I felt real sympathy for. The story is quite dialogue-heavy and might benefit from some judicious editing in this area, but generally the writing is measured, and I enjoyed the subtly of the final paragraphs as Billy struggles with the ghosts of his parents and his past.

HIGHLY
COMMENDED

The Golden Thread

by Rachel Wood

"The tour will start in five minutes," I heard the guide say.
A girl in an old woollen dress sat with bare feet at my table.
"Are you going on the tour?" I asked.

"I live here," she said.

"Oh, I see," I said.

"Yes, I am looking for my threads, they are gold if you find them. I need them. Please, please bring them if you can," she begged.

"I will," I said and smiled at her. Perhaps she was homeless, she looked out of place.

The room was light and bright with, clean wood floors and white inviting tables. Sun shone through the window making the space seem larger. I picked up the small china cup and sipped.

"Good evening everyone, welcome to the Kinda Kafe, I will be your guide for the tour of our Norwich under croft. Can anyone guess what is beneath us?"

A few people nodded.

"Shops and an old street," said a man.

"That's right, but first there is a room, I don't want to spoil the surprise so let's just go down. Mind the steps and the low beams. I haven't lost anyone on the tour yet so don't worry but do take care on the steps. There is a rail so hold on to that and take your time."

We took each step one by one till we reached a room.

"Standing here," said the guide, "you can smell the musty smell of history, it makes me feel excited."

"We are standing in an eighteenth-century weaver's room,"

said the guide. "They had a big window to let in maximum light during the day. They only used tallow candles which smelt and didn't give off much light. There would have been a wooden loom here taking up the space by the window. A family would have worked and lived here. At the side of the building is a Quaker burial ground where the weaver's family was buried which is worth a visit too. There is a ghost that lives here, sometimes we hear a girl crying and knocking on the weaver's window sometimes children running below us in the street."

I felt a bit of a shiver as she spoke. I turned and was sure I saw the outline of a big loom with wooden paddles and metal shafts. There seemed to be a man sitting at the loom with a mass of threads waiting to be woven.

There was a sigh, a rustle in the corner but when I looked again there was nothing.

"Next we will walk through this door into another age," said the guide.

We took our time down the stone steps down to a covered street.

"In the 13 century," said the guide "they dug soil out of a large ditch to create the castle mound. These shops were built in that ditch at the time of Henry VIII. Look up," said the guide "you can see the weaver's window just above us."

I looked up and saw a faint light in the weaver's window and there I was sure I could make out a figure sitting by the window and hear the fast clack of a loom.

We walked along the street, past the shops. I peered through the thick wood window with bent ancient nails. Sitting on a rough stone table was a skein of golden thread. I ignored the sign "no access beyond this point".

I felt cold. "If you see the threads, she had said I need them."

I stepped into the shop, took the silk and quickly hid it beneath my jacket, hardly breathing. I looked around but everyone was listening to the guide.

"There was no sanitation and no running water, they just threw piss pots out into the street. Can you imagine the smell? The shop fronts have changed over the years but the back wall that's original, that's 14th century."

I gazed at the whitewashed walls and the thick wooden beams. What was it like to live in this street, I wondered?

I heard the sound of hurried footsteps in the street. Standing there was the girl in the woollen dress.

She took my hand, she seemed younger than before.

"Come this way," she said.

We stepped into the shop, first her foot, leg and then her whole body began to disappear through the ancient wall.

"Hold on to my hand and you will be fine," she called.

Numbed, I stepped forward feeling ice cold and tingling throughout my body and a great wind in my head.

We had stepped into the weaver's room. Light was streaming through the big window. The first thing that struck me was the smell. The odour of sawdust, spit and tallow and piss seemed to rise from the floor. It was strangely mixed with lavender. On the bedding was a small ginger cat curled up asleep.

"We all sleep here," said the girl, "even Arty cat."

An older man sat on the high wooden seat of the loom his feet working the paddles. His hands were moving so quickly I couldn't see how he worked. He was wearing a wool overshirt and trousers but no shoes. He looked so thin, so thin and gaunt I could hardly see how he had the strength to work the loom for it required a lot of strength, I could see that.

"Is she here then, the lass," he said without pausing his fingers on the fine threads.

"Aye pa she's here right enough and she has the threads, I seen her tek em,"

"Well then there's hope," he said.

"Sit down lass sit down and take some ale by the fire." I sat on the three-legged stool by the small hearth.

"This here is Elizabeth and I be Tom, Tom the weaver."

Elizabeth took the small brush and swept up all the ashes. She threw them through the window down into the street below. Seeing my look of surprise she said, "I cover up the piss so when we walk it don't smell so much. I likes your coat missus. It's a soft material not like any I ever wove."

I treasured my jacket, bought from the middle aisle of Lidl, soft with a hood, practical, comfortable, just £9.99. A bargain I had thought.

"I like it too," I said "Try it on."

Elizabeth draped it round her shoulders and felt the material and then danced round the room.

"Stop that and make the fire and pour that ale," said Tom.

Carefully Elizabeth laid the fire with small pieces of wood and two bits of coal. She took the candle from above the fireplace, lit a sliver of paper and set the fire alight. I put my hands forward feeling the warmth. Elizabeth found 3 clay pots and poured a thick liquid into it. I took a small sip. It tasted sour but it wet my dry mouth. I realised I was shaking.

"So, lass have ye the skeins of silk with you?" Asked Tom "It's good of you to take the trouble."

The cat got up, stretched and rubbed her body round my ankles with a final flourish with her soft tail.

"Yes, yes I have it here somewhere," but when I looked there was no gold skein, the silk had disappeared.

Tom sighed sadly. "I told yun it would na work. We will have to take what's coming to us. The poor house for you and a hanging for me. I watch the hanging from the castle. They let you hang for half an hour they do not snap your drop even then you're not always dead. I see it."

"Oh no!" I said shocked, "surely there is something we can

do."

Elizabeth felt in my jacket pocket and pulled out the gold silken skein.

Tom sighed.

"It's only Elizabeth who can wander through to yons time. She had seen you a few times then you spoke to her and we just hoped. Elizabeth saw the skein in your time but could not touch it. She cannot touch anything there. She likes the company of watching the people with all their talking and laughing. She means no harm just being a girl. Bless you lass we are so grateful."

Tom threaded the silk onto the loom. His hands soon had the silk in place lifting the shafts and the weave began to grow again.

"I'll tell yon lass how it is, our story. We be weavers by trade and good ones too. My father learnt from the Dutch traders. We weave on the back of the cloth and sell our cloth to the wealthy landlords here about for their comfort and warmth. It's fine work. I borrowed money to buy expensive Brussels silks, I had a big commission. Well I know the silk arrived at the docks on the lugger. The man who delivers took a fancy to the gold thread and stole it, so we be 3 skeins short. There be no gold in this cloth. Without it I'd be hung for theft and the loom sold to pay off my debt. Now with your help, given time we will be able to eat and pay the rent again. Do you have the other two skeins?"

"No there was only the one."

"Well lass it's one more than we had."

At that point I heard voices, the tour was returning.

"Back through the weaver's room," said the guide. "Back up to the café for a cup of tea, don't forget to take a look at the burial ground as you go past."

Two people on the tour walked straight into the loom and broke two strands of silk.

108

Tom held up his hands and frowned.

"Them people are allus walking through my weave."

Suddenly I felt impelled to stand up and leave with the tour. It felt painful to leave so unexpectedly without saying goodbye. The room seemed to shrink as I stood at the door. I saw both Tom and Elizabeth recede into the shadows. I stepped into the light of the café. It was a shock to find myself there, I could hardly see. I stumbled out of the door and round the side and into the burial ground. The burial ground was small, walled and full of wildflowers, bees nudging their way into each flower.

I touched each stone to try and get my bearings until I saw the stone Tom Walker weaver of the parish and his daughter Elizabeth.

I felt a soft touch, Arty cat rubbed her head on my hand as I knelt down to feel the stones. She sat on the grave and stared purposefully at me. There in the long grass were the two gold skeins.

I felt so small, so small like a little child and so at peace.

"Arty cat, Arty cat", I heard Elizabeth call.

Seeing me she just smiled, took the skeins from me and disappeared. Arty cat following, her tail straight up in the air.

I could see a cart moving up the street. The loom on top and Tom driving. Elizabeth climbed on the cart.

"Come on lass we are free now; the weave is done, and the rent paid."

They turned into London Street and disappeared.

Adjudicator's feedback: I really enjoyed the local flavour of this glimpse into the history of the weaving trade in Norwich. The movement between past and present is a great idea and allows for some thoughtful juxtapositions between they ways we lived then and now. This is one of the only stories where the 'spooks' weren't frightening or threatening, instead used to illuminate the past with sympathetic, intriguing detail. However, I would suggest revisiting the dialogue belonging to the tour guide, which for me was rather a conspicuous narrative device for describing historical facts, standing out against the more subtle nature of the rest of the story.

Boris and the Boy

by Phyllida Scrivens

@BBCNews@BBCPolitics Dateline: 20 July 2020. Work continues on the restoration of Houses of Parliament. PM Boris Johnson vows, "I am the Captain of this ship. I will be the last to leave."

Prime Minister Johnson surveys the ever-increasing mountain of paper on his leather embossed desk. He knows the workmen will be taking their morning break very soon and longs for respite from the interminable racket. Only another week or so in this section, the Foreman has assured him. Another deafening thud shakes the room and before nothing but the blessed sound of silence. However, before Boris can settle down to work, his thoughts are disturbed by a thin voice within the room, the words interrupted by a persistent cough.

'Sir, sorry Sir, but are you Mr Gladstone Sir?'

Directly in front of him on the rug, sits a small boy, his chin resting on bony knees; a filthy shirt of thick rough cotton cloth draped over narrow shoulders. No more than eight or nine. Emaciated face framed by long tangled hair, thin limbs, his blue eyes sore and inflamed, barely visible through a blackened face.

Despite a rare sensation of alarm, Boris holds his nerve. Very little fazes him nowadays and he is quite comfortable with telling fibs.

'Might be, might be. Who wants to know?'

Twenty minutes earlier Boris had no inkling that the pattern of his day was about to change. Disconcerted by the latest mutiny from amongst his backbenchers, the fifth disruption since he took office in July 2019, Boris strolled to the glazed window, admiring the magnificence of Westminster Abbey.

He could thank his old school chum Dave Cameron for this. The sly old fox had turfed out four Welsh MPs from this suite of offices in 2016, following his resignation from the top job. Stunning chandeliers, green flock wallpaper and the best view in the House. Good old Dave. Whatever happened to him?

Boris was startled, when without warning, an eruption of black soot blasted from the brick chimneybreast, settling like a molehill on the faded Iranian rug. 'Most odd', he mused. 'That flue was boarded up decades ago. Must be to do with the building works.'

He returned to his desk, staring at the computer screen, trawling his files for something to help his case against the latest rebellion. If only he had succeeded in achieving his Halloween Brexit, as he'd promised to the nation, then he might have retained more allies. But that woman, that blonde German piece Ursula von der something, had plotted against him, even before her induction as President of the European Commission. Pity really, she has the most attractive smile.

The strange boy answers Boris's initial question with confidence. 'Harry, Sir. Harry Clarke.' His body shakes with each cough and he rubs his eyes as if unused to the light. Boris is intrigued, if a little spooked.

'Pleased to meet you, Master Clarke. What brings you to the office of the PM?'

'Not sure really, Sir. One minute I 'm 'ard at it, the next I'm sittin' in front of the great Mr Gladstone. My gov'nor talks about you all the time.'

'All good I trust.'

'Wouldn't say that Sir.'

Boris chuckles. 'What about your parents?'

'Pa don't work. Lost his leg in the Bhutan War. Ma says at least he come home but he ain't much use to us now.'

'So you 've had to take on lucrative employment eh?'

'Not sure what you mean exactly Sir. But I does know that us climbing boys are proud to be a part of completing the "greatest building London ever saw", well, that's what my gov'nor says anyhow.'

This was all becoming extraordinarily bizarre. Boris types 'Houses of Parliament' into Google, speed-reading the top result.

The current building was commissioned after the Old Palace of Westminster was destroyed by a fire in 1834. By 1870, under Prime Minister William Gladstone, the construction of the 1,100-room Houses of Parliament was complete.

This has to be a wind up. Boris gazes up at the ceiling looking for hidden cameras or microphones. Is he being filmed for some opprobrious twitter feed? Who's behind this? Wretched lefties? Or perhaps the CIA?

The boy continues. 'If I might be so bold Sir, you do look troubled. Sad even.'

'You're a rum one, aren't you lad? Maybe I am.'

Apart from his aides Boris does indeed walk alone in these vast corridors of power. For the duration of the renovation project all the members and their staff have decamped to a converted modern block in Kensington. But having settled into this palatial and historic office, Boris was not keen to join them. Not yet anyhow. His cabinet were a miserable bunch at the best of times. No one ever joined him for a beer or a whisky after meetings.

So who is this child and where is he going with this line of questioning? Boris nervously runs a hand through his mop of unkempt bleached hair. If this is a terrorist attack, then it's the most eccentric yet. It's like a game. But then Boris loves playing games.

'It's never easy being at the top my boy, you ask your boss.'

At his moment, despite his fascination, Boris makes his decision and presses the panic button beneath the desk. The sound is inaudible in this room but Boris knows that all hell will break loose in his staff office. Unaware of this cry for help, the boy stretches all the muscles in his legs out along the rug, raising a cloud of black soot. Boris waves away the polluted air and slides further back in his chair.

'Sorry Sir', apologises the boy. 'No choice, Sir. I feels like I've been stuck with my knees up for, well, simply ages.'

'No problem my dear boy, no problem' replies Boris, finding himself warming to the sorry creature in front of him. On the other hand his own current predicament was becoming increasingly disturbing. Where on earth is everyone? He listens for approaching footsteps from down the corridor but there are none. Only the distinctive sound of that bothersome pneumatic drill starting up again.

The boy's eyes widen in fear, the ear-splitting noise sending him crawling into the keyhole space beneath Boris's desk. 'What's that Sir? he shouts. 'It ain't thunder. I knows thunder. We boys have to get down sharpish when we hears a storm on it's way.'

'No, no. It's just the workforce shoring up this wing. It's slipping into the Thames you know.'

'I 'adn't heard that Sir. Shocking news indeed.' Boris is troubled by the new proximity of the child. When is help coming? He once again discretely presses the button. Meantime he'll keep the boy talking. It means raising the volume.

'If you wouldn't mind returning to the rug we can talk about you.'

Following instructions is commonplace for Harry. He reluctantly crawls back to his original position. Boris is far more comfortable with this intruder at arm's length. 'And who exactly do you work for?'

'Jack Smith, Sir. Master Chimney Sweep of Stepney.'

This kid is well briefed. No hesitation in his replies. Holding eye contact. Apparently secreting no weapon.

'And did this Mister Smith send you here to see me?'

'No Sir. Not at all. I was doin' my thing, when the next minute here I am sitting on your rug.'

'And what exactly is 'your thing?'

'I shimmy up flues, "like a caterpillar" as the Master says. I use my best brush to break up the loose soot and a scraper to chip away the solid bits. Master says I'm his best boy and I'm proud to be so. My bag of soot is always the biggest when we boys all meet up at the yard.'

'That must be dangerous and exhausting work Harry. I hope you are well reimbursed for your labours.'

'You mean am I paid Sir? No, no. But the Master shares out plates of vittles on Sundays and I take mine home to Ma and Pa. We're all 'umbly grateful to Mister Smith for taking me on.'

'And how often do you, as you say, shimmy up a chimney?'

'Oh, maybe five or six times a day. Seven days a week. Sometimes the Master will make us climb faster by lighting small fires in the grate beneath, or poking the soles of our feet with pointed sticks. Some flues are tighter than others. The ones in this building are very narrow, with lots of bends.'

Boris is taken aback at this information, momentarily forgetting about his own precarious situation. This so-called Mister Smith sounds like a bloody Nazi.

The boy's voice drops to a near whisper so Boris can hardly hear him above the racket. 'Last year I helped demolish a wall at 'ammersmith 'ospital where my mate George Baker was stuck for nearly the whole day.'

'Did George make it, dare I ask?'

'No Sir.'

The two of them pause while each considers George and his dreadful demise. At that same moment the sound of the drilling stops. Boris presses for help again – maybe now someone will actually hear the alarm. Shouldn't be long now.

'So, have you lost many friends Harry?'

"Oh yes, Sir. Some are suffocated from sudden falls of soot. Others get stuck like George, never coming out. And we're all poorly a lot of the time with horrid chesty coughs and sometimes we gets boils on our privates. But my Master lets his lads wash in the Serpentine once a month so I'm one of the lucky ones. It's not so bad.'

Somehow Boris doubts that. He is starting to feel unfamiliar emotions, maybe sympathy or even pity? What would his hero Churchill do? Boris has a sudden craving for buttered crumpets and a chilled glass of Pol Roger. Time to close this nonsense down. As he reaches under the desk *again*, there is a loud knock at the door. Finally.

'Come.'

The door is pushed inwards and Boris can just make out the Works Foreman in the gloom of the corridor. Frustrated not to see his six-foot security guard, Boris snaps at him. 'Enter man, don't dilly dally.' Boris turns to check that the threat is still there, but inexplicably, Harry is nowhere to be seen.

Boris is nonplussed. The Foreman steps forward.

'Sorry to disturb you, Prime Minister. But the men have made a discovery and we think you should know straight away.'

'Where's my Private Secretary, man?'

'Inspecting the findings Sir. He told me to come and fetch you.'

Boris is irritated. 'I'll be having words with him. I've been wrestling with a potential national crisis here. So what is this discovery exactly?'

'It's not pleasant Mr Johnson. During the past half hour, when starting to demolish the chimney stack next to your office, one of my men came across a skeleton.'

'A skeleton?'

'Yes, Sir. A child. Jammed in the flue directly above your office, curled up tight with his knees right under his chin. It gave my man quite a scare I can tell you. I'm afraid Union rules state we must down tools immediately until an official enquiry can be carried out.'

Boris grips the edge of his desk, swaying a little, his thoughts racing. Looking the foreman straight in the eye he says, 'Believe it or not man, I rather think I know exactly who he is.'

*****

Later that afternoon Boris researches the history of child chimney sweeps and to his personal satisfaction discovers that The Chimney Sweepers Act, as proposed by Lord Shaftsbury, was passed in 1875, in an attempt to stop child labour. The Prime Minister at the time was a fellow Conservative, Benjamin Disraeli, in his second term of office, a long-time favourite of Queen Victoria. Following the full enquiry, six more skeletons will be excavated from the chimneys of The Houses of Parliament.

Adjudicator's feedback: I loved the topical interpretation of the theme and this was certainly the entry that made me smile the most! It's ambitious to give voice to one of the most scrutinised politicians of our times but the writing here has real confidence and panache and the twist in the subject matter felt original and intriguing. The tone is well balanced between the lightness of the characters and conversation and the depth of the action – very entertaining.

Author Biographies

IAIN ANDREWS

Originally from Glasgow, Iain Andrews is Chairman of the Norwich Writers' Circle. Prior to moving to the area with his wife Ann, he worked in IT Security, a career that allowed him to travel to every continent except Antarctica.

This is the third year in a row that he has reached the top ten in the Olga Sinclair Prize, although this is his first top-three finish. He's been shortlisted in a number of national contests, and has achieved two second places in Writers' Magazine competitions.

Writing this tale of the supernatural wasn't a first for Iain. In 2018 he created the script for a ghostly event held in the Norwich's Guildhall which received critical acclaim. His story of demonic activity on a remote Scottish island written under the alias Robert Chandler, *A Conspiracy of Ravens*, is available on Amazon.

Iain is also the author of a non-fiction work: 'Thomas Bilney: The Norwich Martyr', published by Poppyland Press.

JOSEPH HIPGRAVE

Joseph Hipgrave attends a writing group in north London. This is the second time he has entered a writing competition. The first time was a schools competition in Ireland in 1981.

On that occasion he won a prize, too. He wonders whether some sort of pattern is emerging. Either way he is extremely pleased and proud at being placed second in the 2019 Olga Sinclair Competition.

ALEXANDER SPARROW

Alexander Sparrow is a writer and character comic from Wellington, New Zealand. His past solo shows include *A Collection of Noises, de Sade, Fred From Featherston, ENIGMA,* and *DJ Trump*. His theatre company, Sparrow & Boyle Entertainment, tours nationally, and has won several awards. *Panorama* is his first published short story.

LESLEY BOWEN

Since giving up a career in accountancy to raise her family, Lesley has refocused her time on her lifelong love of writing. She is currently having a break from editing her second novel to write short stories and poetry. She has been published in Writers' Forum magazine. Aside from writing Lesley enjoys running, piano playing and live music. She lives in the Norfolk countryside south-east of Norwich with her husband and two daughters.

REBECCA BURTON

Rebecca Burton lives in Tongham in Surrey, with her long-suffering husband. Having been an avid reader since she was two, she finally plucked up the courage to start telling her own (weird) stories in 2017. After being shortlisted in several competitions, she sold her first story in 2019 to Abyss & Apex zine. She is currently seeking an agent for her first Young Adult novel, while editing her third. When not writing, she enjoys learning to throw (terrible) pottery and attempting to speak French.

LOUISE GOULDING

Louise Goulding lives in Norwich with her husband, their little boy and their secondhand cat. Her writing was published in the Mother's Milk Books 'The Story Of Us' Prize Anthology in 2014; she was commended in the Words And Women 'About' competition in 2014, and in the Mother's Milk Books Writing Prize in 2016. In her spare time, Louise writes flash fiction on Instagram.

ROBERT KIBBLE

Robert lives in Slough and is a committee member of the Slough Writers Group, which has been running for over fifty years.
He is abnormally upset about the lack of a single Russian oligarch with a preference for recreating zeppelins over buying football teams. Aside from a few short story successes, he has written a novella, "The Girl in the Wave", a modern gothic horror set on the beautiful Cornish coastline, available on Amazon.

CATHY RUSHWORTH

Cathy Rushworth lives in Norwich with her family and dog. She is a member of Norwich Writers' Circle and usually writes children's fiction. She has self- published a picture book "The Bear Extraordinaire" with author/illustrator Karl Newson. Cathy is keen to try different genres including travel pieces, flash fiction and humour.

PHILLIP VINE

Phillip Vine is a proud member of the Norwich Writers' Circle.

His book, *Visionary: Manchester United, Michael Knighton and the Football Revolution, 1989-2019,* is in the shops and available online, published by Pitch Publishing.

He is currently working on a novel, *White Horse*, concerning a pilgrimage undertaken by a group of friends, World War One veterans and conscientious objectors, from their Cambridgeshire village to Wembley, to watch the 1923 FA Cup Final, in which another friend is playing for West Ham United.

LOUISE WILFORD

Louise Wilford currently lives in Barnsley in South Yorkshire. She is an English teacher and is studying for a Masters in Creative Writing with the Open University. She has been writing poetry and short stories since childhood and, over the years, has had around a hundred accepted for publication or placed in competitions (and hundreds more rejected!). In 2018 Louise was awarded second prize in the Olga Sinclair Open Short Story Competition for her story, *Scarlett Johannson is the Anti-Christ*. She is currently working on a children's fantasy novel and a novel for grown-ups set in a school sixth form.

RACHEL WOOD

I live in Norwich with my cat Arty. She helps me to write children's stories. I have a poem called Little Feet in Cromer published in an anthology called *Like the sea I think*. I am part of Norwich Writers circle and am really happy to be highly commended for my spooky story called The Golden Thread.

My story is based on the Kinda Kafe where you can see their ancient street.

PHYLLIDA SCRIVENS

Phyllida Scrivens is a former Chairman of Norwich Writers' Circle. She became a published writer in 2016 when Pen and Sword Books published her debut biography, *Escaping Hitler*. Her award-winning group biography, *The Lady Lord Mayors of Norwich,* followed in 2018 and she is currently researching the history of the Thorpe Great Railway Disaster of 1874, an event that took place less than half a mile from her home in Thorpe St Andrew, Norwich.

JOHN PLATTEN

Jon is the winner of the 2019 Orwell Society Dystopian Fiction Prize: The Report is a critique of education policy, to be published in the forthcoming issue of the society's Journal.

His work has been published in anthologies. In Like The Sea I Think, his piece Retiring to a Space-Time Vortex describes ageing in north Norfolk. He is currently working on a 70,000-word memoir which covers the challenges of leading an inner-city secondary school and adjusting to retirement in the 21st century. The work includes school subject-related sections such as Media Studies Assignment - Love Island with Charles Darwin as a pundit - and Sports Fixture: Two Hours of Misery With Your Son – an evening watching Norwich City. An extract can be found in the 2019 UEA MA Creative Writing Anthology, Brand New and [Almost] Entirely True.

He has written for the periodical Curriculum and has had several pieces featured in the Association of School and College

Leaders' magazine, Leader.

Roses are Red, Tulips are Despatched describes the frustrations of trying to purchase a Valentine's Day gift online. It won the 2019 Colin Sutton Cup for Humour.

Adjudicator Biographies

PIERS WARREN

Piers Warren is a novelist, writer and environmentalist. He has travelled the world as the founder of Wildeye, an International School for Wildlife Film-making , has published a number of successful vegan cookery books, and in 2011 he launched his supernatural thriller *Black Shuck: The Devil's Dog*. He now lives in Pembrokeshire in Wales.

HOLLY AINLEY

Holly Ainley has been the Book Department Manager and Book Buyer in Jarrold, the popular Norwich independent department store, since the end of 2018. She has held a number of roles in the publishing business including editorial positions and as Marketing and Operations Manager at Nine Arches Press.

About the Norwich Writers' Circle

In 1943, at the height of World War 2, a small group of enthusiastic creative writers, both amateur and professional, joined together and established Norwich Writers' Circle. The aim of the founders was to "encourage the art and craft of writing and promote good fellowship amongst Norwich and Norfolk writers generally.

The aim remains unchanged and it is in that spirit that our Circle continues to flourish today, with members work representative of a number of diverse literary styles and genres.

Over the years we have welcomed writers such as Louise de Bernieres, D.J. Taylor, Kathryn Hughes, Simon Scarrow George Szirtes, Rachel Hore, Patrick Barkham, Alison Bruce Hayley Long, Heidi Williamson, Keiron Pim, Elly Griffiths and Emma Healey.

We hold workshops and manuscript evenings when members offer constructive feedback to each other's work. Each season we offer opportunities for members and guests to enter in-house competitions, each judged by professional authors with trophies awarded to our most successful writers.

And finally, we are proud of our annual Olga Sinclair Oper Prose competition, with themes drawn from Norwich life now in its fourth year, offering generous cash prizes to winning entrants. In addition members of the NWC have the opportunity for their entries adjudicated for the much-coveted Olga Sinclair Challenge Shield.

For more information please see our website at:

norwichwriters.wordpress.com

Or at facebook.com/Norwich Writers

Or email an enquiry to:
norwichwriters@hotmail.co.uk

About Black Shuck Gin Ltd

Patrick and Sarah Saunders, together with their children Leanne, Nicola and William launched their family run business in 2011 with their award winning Black Shuck Sloe Gin. Since then the Black Shuck range has flourished and is now recognised all over Norfolk and beyond.

In 2014, Black Shuck Sloe Gin was one of 150 products selected from over 10,000 entrants to be awarded the prestigious 3 stars in the 2014 Great Taste Awards.

In 2015, the Fakenham based family, were invited by Elizabeth Truss MP to be one of just 50 DEFRA Food Stars in recognition of its achievements to date and its entrepreneurial potential for future growth.

The arrival of the legendary Black Shuck Gin in 2015 heralded a new era for Gin lovers old and new.   In August 2017 Black Shuck continued to lead the way with the launch of their limited edition Blush Gin infused with Rhubarb and Strawberry.

The Summer of 2018 saw the arrival of Black Shuck Passion Gin. On numerous occasions members of the ever-expanding Black Shuck Tasting panel were summoned to Black Shuck HQ to taste test an extensive selection of trials. The recipe and methods changed many times before all were in agreement that Passion Gin was ready for you. It goes without saying that this sophisticated Gin has been distilled with an abundance of patience, precision and of course Passion.

Black Shuck's Navy Strength Ignite Gin arrived in the Autumn of 2018.

At 57.15% abv Black Shuck Ignite delivers a Gin that is outrageously smooth and unapologetically bold. It is alleged that during the 18th century Rear Admiral Sir Thomas Desmond Gimlette, of the Royal Navy, administered a concoction of gin and lime to help immunise the crew against illnesses such as scurvy and malaria.

With the on-board Gin rations being stored in close proximity to the barrels of gunpowder there was a risk of the gunpowder becoming soaked and rendered useless during rough seas and battle engagements. However, it was recognised that so long as the spirit was sufficiently high in alcoholic strength the gunpowder would still ignite. This same principal was used as a method of establishing 'proof' by the Naval purser who was responsible for all supplies on board. He would test the alcoholic strength by adding a few grains of gunpowder to the spirit. If the compound just ignited it was taken as 'proof' that the spirit was at the correct strength.

In 1816 Bartholomew Sikes invented a hydrometer that measured 100 proof at 57.15% abv. Today the term Navy Strength is used on "proof spirits" that are bottled at between 57% and 58% abv.

This is not a family that likes to sit still and the Summer of 2019 saw the arrival of their Black Shuck Vodka and there is a promise of much more to come before the year is out.

The Black Shuck Team were honoured and delighted to support The Norwich Writers' Circle this year with their creative writing competition.

What is Black Shuck?

THE LEGEND OF BLACK SHUCK

According to English folklore, Black Shuck, a large ghostly spirit dog with malevolent flaming red eyes, has haunted the East Anglian countryside for hundreds or even thousands of years. Many sightings have been recorded particularly along the coastlines, dark lanes and footpaths.

As with all legends, stories of Black Shuck have been told, exaggerated and retold resulting in as many variations of the legend as there are varieties of Gin.

It has been suggested that Sir Arthur Conan Doyle took inspiration from Black Shuck when writing the classic thriller, Hound of the Baskervilles. In 1901 Sir Arthur returned from South Africa suffering from Typhoid Fever. Whilst recovering, he and his companion, Bertram Fletcher Robinson, took a golfing holiday in North Norfolk. They stayed at the Cromer Links Hotel and visited Cromer Hall where Doyle and Robinson, a collector of strange myths and local legends, would undoubtedly have heard chilling tales of the fearsome Black Shuck.

www.blackshuckltd.co.uk

Printed in Poland
by Amazon Fulfillment
Poland Sp. z o.o., Wrocław

53751611R00078